FIRE
in the
WIND

FIRE
in the
WIND

A NOVEL

Dana M. Stein

TATE PUBLISHING & Enterprises

Published by Tate Publishing & Enterprises, LLC
127 E. Trade Center Terrace | Mustang, Oklahoma 73064 USA
1.888.361.9473 | www.tatepublishing.com

Tate Publishing is committed to excellence in the publishing industry. The company reflects the philosophy established by the founders, based on Psalm 68:11,
"The Lord gave the word and great was the company of those who published it."

Published in the United States of America

ISBN: 978-1-61663-342-4
Fiction: Visionary
10.06.09

For Margaret, Elayna and Julianna

Foreword

Anyone who is concerned about climate change—or any environmental or social issue, for that matter—wonders how he or she can make a difference. Environmental issues are so big, so all-encompassing, that it seems hard for any individual to have much impact.

Advocates urge that the impact of individual choices—recycling, conserving energy, using renewable energy—can, when multiplied many times over, change the course of our environment. And that certainly is true, though it seems that we are not yet close to that point when the individual actions of many will reverse our course on global warming.

In my case, I have long thought that one problem in the climate change debate is the difficulty of imagining how day-to-day life could be altered by significant global warming. News stories describe scenarios in which climate change will cause sea levels to rise, new diseases to break out, and storms to grow in magnitude. Already, we hear of how average temperatures have risen; Arctic ice is melting; and some animals' habitat or migration patterns have been affected. Some speculate that Hurricane Katrina, or the deadly heat wave that hit Europe in 2003, could be examples of the dangerous weather events that will become more frequent in the future.

But what's less apparent is how such changes would affect daily life. How will our way of life *really* change? The debate in the media or at international conferences frequently focuses on quantitative matters—how much should each country's emissions be reduced, or how much temperature rise would make catastrophic climate change likely. The occasional exception is also on a grand scale, as when Pacific Island nations plead for action lest their countries slip below rising sea levels. Overall, the debate seems to lack the context of *what will life be like*, if insufficient action is taken.

This disconnect was brought home to me when I discussed climate and energy issues with high school students. If anyone would be worried, I thought, it would be students who will be growing up in a world whose environment may change significantly. Many were indeed concerned, but others expressed surprising skepticism. One student said that climate change's impact was too far in the future to be worried about. Another said that it was difficult to visualize what the world would look like with global warming.

So I have written *Fire in the Wind* in an effort to describe a future that is dominated by climate change. One chal-

Dana M. Stein

lenge was determining what year to place my story in. At first I thought I'd make the year 2052 (it would have to be a presidential election year); but then I realized that, with scientific predictions getting a little more dire every year, I could safely place the story in 2036 and assume that significant climate change was already taking place.

There are many stories in the press about current and future impacts of climate change, but several articles were particularly helpful in imagining a future in which major climate change had set in. The cover stories in the November/December 2002 issue of *Harvard* magazine and the April 3, 2006 edition of *Time* magazine were comprehensive in their descriptions and analysis of future scenarios. The maps found on the MSN web site and in the February 2008 edition of *National Geographic* were helpful in understanding the ramifications of climate change around the world.

Other sources included the article in the January 2008 edition of *Scientific American* entitled "Solar Grand Plan," which was helpful in imagining the potential of photovoltaic farms, and the pamphlet *Central Park Wildlife*, authored by James Kavanagh and Raymond Leung, which I drew on in writing Chapter 10. Also, an energy conservation program described in the book was inspired by the energy-efficiency project of Civic Works, Inc., the Baltimore non-profit organization with which I am affiliated.

There are several people I wish to thank for their assistance on this book. My mother and step-father Elisabeth and Raymond Cook and my wife Margaret reviewed drafts of the book and offered many good suggestions. Steven

Heinl also provided some helpful ideas. Most of all, I must thank my wife for her patience and support. She voiced little dissent during the hours I missed with her and our beautiful daughters, Elayna and Julianna, while I was at the computer. As an educator with an environmental science background, Margaret shares my passion about climate change. She and I agree that it is for our daughters and their generation that we hope for the wisdom and ability to pass on a world better than the one we inherited.

—*Baltimore, Maryland*
August 2009

Dana M. Stein

Chapter 1

The last straw came in the mail on that Friday.

Harry Harper had been expecting the letter for some time and every day had checked his mailbox like a high school senior anxiously awaiting an admissions letter from college.

For the previous week, Harper had tried to keep his mind off the letter and the newest report of the National Academy of Sciences. The report forecasted a bleak future for America's farmers and said that global warming was turning the country from a net exporter of food to an importer for the first time in two centuries.

Harper and his friends had come to call global warming simply "the warming." The group of six life-long farmers from Southeastern Iowa had been meeting at the Roadside Diner in Bloomfield for Friday morning breakfast for more than twenty years. When they first started gathering in the 2010s, the warming hadn't yet come to dominate their lives—they could talk about wheat futures, the latest equipment at the John Deere store, and how ornery the milk cows had been that morning. There had been a slight increase in average temperatures in Iowa, but for the most part, the threats Harper had to deal with were the same ones farmers had faced for a long-time— whether there would be enough rain, what price their crops would fetch, how long they could use spare parts to keep their farm machinery going.

All that had changed by the early 2030s. Now, when Harper and friends met for their regular Friday mélange of eggs, bacon, and hash browns, the tone of their conversation was darker. Every week they focused on the latest prediction of what the warming was going to do to their crops, and which friend had lost his farm to the warming. The waitress who poured their coffee would sometimes stop to listen to their discussions. She said their somber conversations made it sound as if "the warming" was a relentless, sci-fi creature that couldn't be stopped.

In a sense, it was. Every time farmers thought they had dealt with one of the changes caused by the warming, a new one appeared. Recent years had brought intense storms that could dump more than three inches of rain in a single day. Although freshly-planted crops would frequently perish under the onslaught, farmers could save their mid-summer crops by building costly drainage systems around their fields.

Harper didn't mind having to install the drainage system too much, if for no other reason than it reminded him of the fancy ballpark he had seen in Chicago. Every few

Dana M. Stein

months he would have to drive to meet with the banker who held the mortgage on his farm. The meetings with the banker, Fred Wilmer, weren't particularly productive, since Wilmer would usually scratch his head and wonder how Harper would be able to keep up with his monthly payments. But the one relaxing part of the trip was that after his meetings with Wilmer, Harper would usually be able to take in a baseball game at Wrigley Field. He still loved watching his Cubs, the team he had grown up with, and he marveled at the new baseball field. After even a big cloudburst of rain, the underground drainage pipes would suck away the rain, and the ballgame would be played. He enjoyed those trips to the ballpark, since they reminded him of the many times he and his son Brian had whiled away long summer nights watching baseball. He thought about 2015, the year that the Cubs broke one of baseball's longest curses and had won the World Series. Years later, Harper found something comforting in watching a game whose format and rules and rhythms had not changed very much in almost 200 years. With everything else changing around him, any ritual or routine was important.

But the heavy rains that plagued the early 2030s were gradually replaced by a completely different phenomenon: drought. Initially, before the drought became severe, Harper had been able to convert his fields from corn to sorghum, which was a hardier crop and could grow in warmer temperatures. For a few years, the plan worked. Harry didn't have to worry about his fields being battered by freak storms, and he was able to salt a little money away for next year.

But as 2034 ended, the drought intensified. After a

while, there was little Harper and his pals could do. No amount of irrigation could save their crops. Sometimes his sorghum could hang on until the fall, when there was some relief from the poor rainfall. But in 2035, Southern Iowa became prey to blinding heat waves that would top 100 degrees, more than twenty degrees above normal summer highs. When that happened, his sorghum shriveled into brown stumps. His farm, which had been passed down through eight generations of Harpers, was withering away.

Slowly but surely, the Friday morning group at the Roadside Diner grew smaller. One of Harper's oldest friends, Judd Swenson, lost his farm of fifty years and had no choice but to swallow his pride and move in with his children in Des Moines. Another friend, George Metheny, whose health had never been good, suffered a stroke when the drought began and was confined to a nursing home. Those who still showed up on Friday mornings talked about the rumors of farmer suicides in Missouri, where the drought had started in 2033, before creeping north to Iowa.

With the drought decimating their farms, their only hope had been to apply to the National Global Warming Relief Agency. The agency had been set up to process farmers' claims for compensation from the changes wrought by the warming. Every year, as more and more farmers sent in applications, the standard the agency used to process claims had stiffened. It used to be that if the warming had lowered the value of farms, the owners could claim compensation. Now, the agency said that farmers could get relief only if the property decline was not "reasonably foreseeable," whatever that meant.

That attitude had upset many farmers. In the early 2030s, the U.S. Department of Agriculture had pleaded with family farmers to resist the urge to sell their farms and get out of the business. USDA had told them that the government was researching drought-resistant crops, and that if they hung in there, they would be fine. People like Harper had resisted the offers of agribusiness to buy their farms, out of a vague sense of patriotism or sheer stubbornness. Of course, the fire sale prices the huge corporate farms were offering got his dander up really bad too.

After reading the letter one more time, he put it down and took a deep breath. He opened up his closet, where at the top was a box that hadn't been opened for some time. He pulled it down, carefully put it on the table, and opened it. There inside was the .38 caliber pistol he had bought years ago, but which he'd never used, not even for target practice. He stared at it for several minutes, and then put it in his pants pocket. After he put the box back in the closet, he left the house and locked the front door. He took a long look at the dusty fields of the farm, the site his family had called home since the 1820s, slid into the front seat of his pickup, and started driving down the path to the main road.

Chapter 2

The phone rang just after five in the morning. Michael Baines, never an early riser, picked up the receiver, dropped it, and finally intoned a groggy, "Hello." It was his boss, the President's national security advisor, informing him that a ski lodge in Colorado had been bombed overnight. Several people had been killed. His boss—a gruff older man named D'Alesio—said that the bombing had the fingerprints of DOE, the Defenders of Earth, all over it. Baines protested a little, saying that DOE had pledged non-violence just last month, but D'Alesio cut him off and told him to get in extra early for a meeting of the National Security Council. Eight a.m., Baines's normal arrival time, was much too early as it was, so he didn't relish the idea of heading in even sooner.

His apartment was spare—befitting an overworked White House aide who was rarely home—and as he

Dana M. Stein

stumbled around searching for his clothes, he almost knocked over the few pictures he had on his dresser. One was of the Grand Canyon, which he had hiked after he graduated law school. Unlike his law school friends, who leisurely traipsed through Europe after taking the bar exam, he and a friend had hiked to the canyon's bottom in the August heat. He had barely made it back up to the canyon's southern rim, but after being passed on the trail by a seventy-five-year old, he had found the energy to complete the trek. Though the trip had tested his physical limits, he had loved seeing the changing colors of the rocks and the shooting stars at night. There was a simple majesty about the Grand Canyon that left Baines in awe. He remembered that the canyon made him feel that Mother Nature was indomitable, an impression that now seemed somewhat archaic.

The other photo was of his family, from when his mother was still alive. He loved the picture because everyone—Baines's parents, his little sister Abigail, and he—seemed to be happy. His mother provided the ballast that kept the family on an even keel, and the photo had been taken the month before she was diagnosed with cancer.

It was when he glanced at the photo that he remembered the dream he'd had that night. He'd been having some intense dreams recently, but the dream from that night was one of the rare pleasant ones. Baines's father had owned a power boat when he was a teenager, and Baines's dad, Abigail, and he loved to zoom around the inlets near their home on the Chesapeake Bay. In his dream, Baines's father had finally let him take charge of the boat, and Baines was in heaven. He took them to small hidey-holes that they'd never seen before and he took them to a small island where he and his sister ran around until they collapsed with exhaustion. It was a nice dream, Baines thought.

By the time Baines was ready to leave his apartment, it was six-thirty. He opened his refrigerator to get some orange juice or milk, but the shelves were bare. *Damn,* Baines thought, he had forgotten to program his new fridge to automatically e-mail a delivery order to the grocery store when he ran out of the few staples he kept on hand. He quickly adjusted the refrigerator's settings and grabbed his well-worn briefcase. It was late September, so by the time Baines left his apartment, dawn was just breaking.

On early mornings like this one, Baines appreciated the sensors that automatically turned off the lights and air conditioning when he locked the door to his apartment. They were part of the national efficiency campaign designed to slash home energy use. At first Baines thought the sensors were odd—it was almost as if his apartment had a mind of its own—but on days like today, when he was only half-awake as he got ready for work, he appreciated any economy of effort.

Baines thought for a second about skipping his regular morning detour, but he decided that he had to see his father. His father was one of the many who were "the displaced." When rising sea levels started lapping at their front doors, many of the displaced on the East Coast had headed to the nearest town or city, looking for whatever higher land could be found. For tens of thousands of peo-

Dana M. Stein

ple, that meant in the end living out of a trailer, or even pitching a tent, in one of the large resettlement areas that the Department of Homeland Security had set up outside cities. These areas had become known as "Coopervilles," after the former president who had pledged that no American would ever be displaced by the rising tide.

Baines's father was in a somewhat different category. He hadn't lost his home to the warming, but his livelihood was gone. He was a member of the last generation of Chesapeake Bay crabbers and oystermen. The Bay had struggled to maintain its shellfish population during the first part of the twenty-first century, with some progress being made against the nutrient pollution and runoff that contaminated the water. That was until Hurricane Alberta. When Alberta roared into the Bay in 2035, its turbulence wiped out most of the crabs and oysters that people like Baines's dad depended on. Rising sea levels had weakened the coastline's natural defenses of wetlands and tidal areas, so that Alberta's punch was able to reconfigure the outline of much of the Bay.

Thousands of homes were lost, but those protected by the government's sea walls had survived mostly intact. There had been a long-simmering anger over which coastal communities got the walls and which did not—the fortunate ones tended to be the more upscale communities—and after Alberta, this anger turned to a boil. Some of the displaced decided they would take their protest to Washington, D.C., and Baines's father decided that he had nothing better to do than to join them.

When the group of 200 or so got to the White House

and demanded a reception with President Hartwell, they instead got a meeting with an aide who told them that the President was too busy. The aide—who in addition to being impertinent and condescending, was about half their average age—provided little balm for the disquiet of the protesters. They purchased some tents and pitched them on the National Mall, right next to the Washington Monument and in full view of the Lincoln Memorial. How long they would stay there, they didn't know, but it was better than going back to lost homes and livelihoods.

Baines's apartment was right off Pennsylvania Avenue on Seventh Street, so he didn't have a long walk to the Mall. Even before 7 a.m., a humid haze was visible over the Capitol building. Washington in late September was still in the grip of summer weather, with temperatures regularly topping eighty-five degrees. Over the years, as average temperatures had slowly climbed, the mugginess that made Washington infamous had only gotten worse.

Baines thought about the gradual changes that Washington had experienced as temperatures grew hotter. Instead of blooming in March, as they had for more than a century, Washington's famous cherry blossoms now bloomed in February. Then there were the changes less visible from Pennsylvania Avenue, such as the resettlement camp that had been set up for people displaced by the rising Anacostia River. Baines had never visited it, but conditions supposedly were squalid in the camp. A recent storm had caused the Anacostia, always a polluted river, to overflow its banks and flood the camp, causing an outbreak of hepatitis. *If there was any silver lining to global warming*, Baines thought, *it*

Dana M. Stein

was that winter snowstorms in Washington were now a rarity.
Since the mere threat of a few inches of snow usually had
caused Washingtonians to react with mild panic, the near-
disappearance of snow wasn't such a bad thing.

As he walked across Pennsylvania Avenue, Baines
looked down the long, wide boulevard. He never tired of
looking at the stately government buildings that lined the
street. He had finally gotten used to the sight of solar panels atop the Justice Department and other federal buildings. With declining oil production pushing the cost of oil
past $500 per barrel, solar panels were now ubiquitous in
most cities. Even in low-lying Washington, D.C., which
originally had been built on top of a swamp, some buildings had mini-wind turbines on their rooftops.

When Baines reached the Mall, he looked for his dad's
gray tent, which was among the hundreds of green, blue,
and gray tents that speckled the Mall. He soon found his
dad, who was up and about and boiling water for coffee.
His father was a tall man with sinewy arms developed from
years of crabbing. Baines had his dad's height but not his
strength or physicality, which meant that from an early
age Baines didn't want to pursue his father's trade. It was
not that Baines looked down on his dad's work; it was just
that he wanted to do something different. His dad, however, interpreted Baines's dislike for crabbing as disdain. So
while the two had been close during Baines's early years,
that closeness had dissipated as Baines grew older.

That morning, his dad had been reading a history of
the Mall. He commented how Baines should wake up
early and read by the dawn's early light—it was calming

and took his mind off his troubles. Baines just grunted, wondering if he and his dad really had the same DNA.

Then he told Baines about an interesting item that he'd read that morning. He and his tent-mates were on the same ground as the Poor People's Campaign, whose participants had camped out on the Mall in protest of the nation's poverty in 1968. They had come from all over the country, with some traveling by mule train, and had called their camp "Resurrection City." Baines, who prided himself on his knowledge of American history, confessed he didn't know that. Baines's dad wondered how the 1968 protesters would react if they saw the poverty of the Coopervilles.

"Today's conditions might be worse than they were seventy years ago," he added.

"I don't know; 1968 was a terrible time, the country was in turmoil and we lost some great leaders," Baines replied.

"At least they had good leaders back then, better than that boss of yours," Baines's dad sniffed.

"Dad, you know I wish the President would show more gumption on a lot of things, including the warming."

"Then why do you stay with him?"

"Things are complicated; they aren't black and white. Look, I just hope you have more luck with your protest than your twentieth-century forerunners had," Baines shot back. "Anyway, do you have enough food for the rest of the week?"

"Enough to get by," was the reply. Some church volunteers had dropped off canned goods and a new microwave that was solar powered.

"Son, you waste your time worrying about me. You

forget that I survived plenty of storms on the Bay when I was crabbin.' But there is one thing you can help me and the other folks here with—be sure to tell that president of yours to keep his Park Police off this camp, you hear? Last night there was another scare when we saw a bunch of policemen on horseback circling the Mall."

"Yeah, I'll be sure to tell him myself," Baines snapped back. "You just take care of yourself. And any day you decide you'd rather sleep on a nice sofa rather than the federal government's turf, you know where my apartment is."

"I'm not leaving my buddies, and you know that. So just go to work and leave me to my book."

It was time to go—to leave his father alone and make the NSC meeting—so Baines and his father hugged awkwardly, and Baines walked the short distance to the White House. He passed through the wrought-iron gate and the bushes with multiple hidden cameras, and entered the door. As he produced his ID and passed through the retina scan, the White House's newest security measure, he thought about what his father had said about leaders. He wished that with all of the troubles of the country, the current occupant of the Oval Office would get some spine and show some leadership on climate change. He didn't know if it would happen, but he could hope.

He opened the door to the national security meeting room and entered what he knew would be a difficult meeting.

Chapter 3

It was 9:45 a.m., and Professor Emma Margolis readied her notes for today's lecture in her class, ENV 230, The Science and Politics of Global Warming. Over the years, it had become one of the most popular classes at New York University, and this year Margolis was teaching to an overflowing classroom.

Margolis was tired, having recently returned from a trip to the Arctic. She was studying the feedback mechanisms of climate change and had traveled with the USS *Pennsylvania*, a nuclear submarine that went every year to the North Pole to measure the thickness of the Arctic ice. That summer had been the first in which the Arctic ice cap had completely disappeared. By mid-September, parts of the ice cap had re-emerged, but Margolis was able to calculate that the polar sea ice had lost 80% of its average thickness since 1950.

As the *Pennsylvania* meandered past the North Pole and out into the North Atlantic, its crew had discovered an impressive, daunting sight: flotillas of huge icebergs. As Greenland's ice slowly melted, it sloughed off hundreds of ice mountains that wended their way south. One of the *Pennsylvania's* crew members commented to Margolis that his great-grandfather had been a Navy look-out for German U-boats in that same part of the Atlantic during World War II. By contrast to Nazi submarines, he thought, icebergs were a much more benign threat, but they still were sinister—once it melted in warmer waters, each iceberg would contribute to the slowly rising sea level that was threatening America's way of life.

But for now, Margolis had to focus on her upcoming lecture. The main topic of the class would be the new National Academy of Sciences report, but she knew that students would want to discuss the Colorado bombing and its impact on the presidential election that was less than two months away. While her reputation as a DOE sympathizer had spread among the faculty, she wasn't sure if her students had picked up on it.

As she crossed New York University's grounds to the lecture hall, the campus seemed abuzz. The New York dailies had splashed the news of the bombing across their front pages, and NYU was known as a hotbed of environmental fervor. New York University had affiliates of every mainstream-to-radical environmental group, and students regularly filled nearby Washington Square Park demanding more action on climate change. Once, a student had grabbed the scabbard held by the statue of the soldier Giuseppe Garibaldi and started a march on the school's administration building. NYU's president had frantically called upon Margolis, known for having a good rapport with students, to stop the march, which she did after running to the park, climbing atop some steps, and pleading with the students through a bullhorn. She also got the scabbard back from the wayward student.

Margolis quickly arrived at the lecture hall. A petite woman barely five feet tall, she squeezed her way through the standing-room-only crowd in the classroom. Margolis announced that while she was going to talk about the new Academy report, she knew that wasn't the item that everyone wanted to discuss.

Her students didn't disappoint her. They pummeled her with questions about the bombing and its implications. The students seemed evenly divided as to whether DOE was responsible or not. Some believed that DOE was sincere in its declaration to abandon violence as a means to promote its drastic solutions to global warming. Others believed that DOE's truce was a temporary one, aimed at garnering support for the proposed congressional ban on gas-powered engines.

Margolis professed agnosticism as to whether DOE was involved in the bombing, and instead steered the class toward a discussion of its political impact. "How does this affect the likelihood of the ban's passage?" she asked. One student claimed with utter certitude that this meant the death-knell of the ban. Congressional fence-sitters will think that by supporting the ban, they're supporting environmental terrorists, he claimed. Others thought that by

Dana M. Stein

quickly deploring the attack, ban supporters could still garner enough votes.

Margolis then asked about the presidential race, which up until that time seemed to slightly favor the re-election of the incumbent, President Hartwell, over his Republican challenger, Senator Bingham. Hartwell was reluctant to endorse the ban, for fear of alienating swing voters in Midwest states that still had automobile plants. Many plants had closed—between the two remaining U.S. manufacturers, General Motors and Ford, they had less than forty percent of the American market—but the car companies and the auto union still had political clout.

Still, Hartwell was seen as more supportive of anti-global warming efforts than his opponent. Early in his term, he had signed into law a bill that outlawed "gas guzzlers" and increased the national renewable portfolio standard—which mandated the percentage of power that had to come from renewable sources—to 50% by 2045.

Bingham, by contrast, based his global warming strategy almost entirely on new technologies that might reduce the levels of atmospheric carbon. While efforts to increase the ocean's absorption of carbon dioxide had failed up to now, he advocated new proposals to create huge algae blooms in the oceans and to seed the atmosphere with particles that reflected sunlight.

On this issue, students were almost uniformly of the belief that Hartwell would be hurt by the Colorado attack. They based their argument on what had happened during the first two decades of the century when the U.S. was still engaged in a war against Middle East terrorists.

Twice, when a centrist or liberal candidate seemed to be on the verge of winning the presidency, terrorist groups had launched an attack overseas or released an ominous video, which always produced a bounce in the polls for the hard-line candidate. Since most people in the country viewed DOE as an environmental terrorist group, Margolis's students thought the Colorado attack would produce the same result.

"Very interesting," Margolis mused. "Time will tell if you get an 'A' in political prognostication. But since this class is about both politics *and* science," she said, "let's get to the science part.

"Most of you have heard by now of the new National Academy of Sciences study. But what exactly does it say?"

"It concludes that global warming is accelerating. Worldwide temperatures have already risen by an average of two degrees Fahrenheit, and another degree rise is forecast during the next ten years. The main reason for the acceleration, according to the study, was that the feedback loop between ice melt and warming was stronger than expected.

"The feedback loop is something I recently witnessed with my own eyes. You may have heard that I just returned from the frozen yonder. I had the opportunity to travel in a U.S. submarine, packed with nuclear-tipped missiles, under the North Pole." She impressed her students as she pulled out a large, glossy print of the *Pennsylvania* bursting through the sea. "It was a great learning experience, though one I don't think I'll repeat anytime soon; you never know how claustrophobic you are until you spend days in a submarine.

"Anyway, years ago, in the summertime, there would be plenty of polar ice. Now, there is nothing in July and August. As disconcerting as that is, what is worse is that the open sea is worsening climate change. As you know, ice reflects sunlight, while ocean water absorbs almost all of it. That creates a powerful interaction that is accelerating the pace of global warming."

Margolis continued with her description of the trip. "After the *Pennsylvania* dropped me off in Newfoundland, I trekked inland to Quebec province, to take a look at how Canada's peat is doing. The answer is, not well. Peat is full of carbon dioxide, but it's been preserved in the ground by damp and cold conditions. But with rising temperatures, these conditions are slowly disappearing. That means that the peat is gradually becoming combustible, creating a risk of enormous releases of CO_2. In fact, there have been a few fires already, though fortunately the Canadians have been nimble enough to contain them.

"All of this means that the feedback loop is overwhelming the world's efforts to reduce man-made CO_2 emissions. Through more efficient cars, buildings, and power plants, the industrialized world has finally started to reduce its CO_2 output significantly. But because of the melting ice, the oceans are getting warmer, which melts more ice, which raises sea level and further increases water temperature. Also, methane is now a major problem. The melting of the permafrost in northern latitudes is releasing huge quantities of methane into the atmosphere.

"So what does the National Academy report say about the ramifications? Storms will continue to be more frequent and stronger. The type of level five hurricane that struck Southeast Florida in 2032 will become more frequent. With many thousands of the displaced crowding East Coast cities in substandard housing, the potential for catastrophic loss of life, as happened in Miami, will increase.

"Not surprisingly, the additional temperature rise will further increase sea levels and precipitate more drought. Already, the half-meter rise in sea levels that early twenty-first century scientists predicted has happened more quickly than most had forecast. Another half-meter rise is likely by 2055, further eroding coastlines along the East Coast and the Gulf Coast. The report recommends the abandonment of New Orleans during the next decade.

"The drought that's laid waste to parts of the Midwest farm belt will only intensify. The U.S. will lose our distinction of being the breadbasket of the northern hemisphere, as more farms are abandoned. America's farming loss will be Canada's gain, with formerly marginal farms in Canadian provinces becoming more productive as temperatures rise."

When a student asked what the additional sea level rise meant for New York City, Margolis said the report didn't say and she couldn't predict. Right now, the southern tip of Manhattan was effectively closed off to the public due to frequent flooding. At minimum, the wall that protected the financial district from the Hudson River would have to be bolstered.

As Margolis wrapped up her analysis of the report, she came to what was perhaps the most ominous part. The impact of global warming was spreading in new, less predictable ways. For decades, scientists could reliably predict that temperatures and sea levels would rise; what was uncertain was how quickly this would happen. Now, scientists were seeing changes in ocean currents that at one time were thought to be very unlikely. For example, the warm Atlantic currents that maintained a temperate climate in Northern Europe were shifting. Great Britain, Ireland, and the northern countries of continental Europe could see a marked chilling in climate. As the U.S. becomes a net food importer due to drought, Europe could seek food imports because of longer winters. Food prices, which had escalated dramatically in recent years, would climb even higher.

By the time Margolis concluded, there was dead silence in the classroom. "Well, I can see I've scared a lot of people. Not everything is doom and gloom. The National Academy report states that warmer temperatures are creating more cloud cover, and these tend to be clouds that reflect sunlight. That will help in offsetting the feedback loop we've discussed. Also, the report says that some climate change countermeasures may have promise. We'll talk about those in our next class."

Her few optimistic words didn't lift the pall of quiet that had settled over the room. As the class ended and students got up to leave, the classroom chatter that had started the lecture was now gone. Students talked quietly as they tried to absorb what they had learned.

Chapter 4

Baines settled into his seat at the huge conference table that was used for full meetings of the NSC. He had started in late 2033 as a junior NSC member. For the past two years his duties had focused on monitoring overseas developments relating to global warming. Initially he had kept track of the growing misery in Third World countries as rising temperatures changed agricultural patterns. Several countries in South America and semiarid parts of Africa had been particularly hard hit by drought and resulting famine. The U.S. had initially contributed substantial amounts of relief, but with growing concern about reduced crop production in the Midwest, Congress had cut off the supply of grain relief.

As international complications expanded, his portfolio grew as well. Tensions in South Asia had simmered as the receding glaciers caused conflict over water supply. In

2035, India and Pakistan massed troops on their border as the countries quarreled over rights to diminished water supplies. Baines had joined the Secretary of State in a mediation that had produced a temporary resolution, but he worried that it wouldn't last long.

Then there was the terrible monsoon that wiped out part of Dhaka in Bangladesh. The low-lying city had already suffered significant erosion due to rising sea levels, which only made the impact of the monsoon that much worse. Baines was in charge of U.S. disaster relief in Dhaka, and while he had visited Miami and New Orleans after their hurricanes, he had never seen such misery as he witnessed in what remained of the slums of Dhaka.

In early 2036, Baines also became the U.S. liaison to the United Nations Committee on Environmental Refugees, which assisted with the resettlement of individuals who had been displaced by more frequent hurricanes and slowly-rising sea levels. The U.S. had refused U.N. aid with respect to its own environmental refugees, but was willing to help the displaced in other countries. Baines had been on location as the residents of the Pacific island country of Palau said good-bye to their disappearing country. He had also assisted island residents of the Canadian province of British Columbia relocate, just as Alaskan Inuit villagers had slowly lost their homes to the melting coastal ice.

Given the international focus of his work, he was surprised when D'Alesio walked into his office early in 2036 to announce that his duties were changing. D'Alesio told him that with the rise in domestic unrest and the upcoming presidential election, he was being put on the team that coordinated the White House response to domestic developments relating to climate change. When Baines complained that he had little experience in politics, D'Alesio grunted that he'd learn, and besides, there was little the U.S. could do to help the poor bastards in the Third World cope with global warming.

Baines really disliked his new assignment. He had not met many politicians he admired, and always chafed at the idea of sacrificing sound policy for political judgments. He knew that the President worried about his chances for re-election, and thought Hartwell would throw good climate change policy overboard if it meant he could pick up a few more electoral votes. Indeed, the subtext for almost all of the NSC's deliberations was how the swing states in the Midwest and Northwest would be affected by policy decisions. The near-impossibility of achieving consensus among bickering federal agencies on global warming policy made Baines's job even more unpalatable.

It was unusual for the President to attend an NSC session, but today he was there, sitting at the head of the table. Baines didn't think Hartwell was the brightest bulb in the group, but he could command attention. "Good morning," Hartwell said in his stentorian tones, "though I hardly think this morning qualifies as a good one. Just when I think we're on track with this global warming issue, we're thrown off track by this damn bombing."

"Mr. President," chimed in D'Alesio, "there is every indication that this is the work of the DOE outlaws." Baines winced, but said nothing. "The *Denver News-Post* received the usual claim of responsibility from

DOE," D'Alesio continued. "Most people thought their announcement last month of a cease-fire in their so-called 'actions' was a deception, and I think, Mr. President, this sadly confirms it."

The President was not inclined to disagree. "And our response to this?"

"You must denounce the bombing, DOE, and their effort to interfere with the presidential election and the congressional hearings."

Hartwell asked, "Any indication that this could be the start of a series of attacks?"

D'Alesio turned to Baines to respond. "Usually, Mr. President, DOE would have a quick succession of attacks, but up to now their actions have resulted in no deaths," Baines said. "Given the unique nature of this bombing, I don't think we can predict if there will be more attacks."

Hartwell was skeptical. "I think they'll hit again. Be sure to step up our surveillance of their leadership. Do we need to keep getting approvals for new wiretaps from that useless court? Can't we just go ahead and do it?"

"I'm sorry, Mr. President," the White House counsel replied. "You'll remember that members of our own party said we'd violated the Congressional law on wiretapping after the first wave of DOE attacks."

"Yes, I remember that all too well," Hartwell snapped. "Look, I just want to look strong on this issue of eco-terrorism. The election has gotten much too close." The President took a long breath. "And I've decided that I will consider signing the congressional ban if it passes, but I'll only do it if DOE doesn't stir things up anymore."

Several heads immediately turned toward the President. "Mr. President," the Chairman of the Joint Chiefs sputtered, "if you sign the ban, your opponents may claim that you're caving into DOE. I thought you were going to oppose the ban, or at least wait until after the election to decide about it."

"Yes, that's what I'd said," Hartwell answered. "But this new Academy of Sciences report shows we need to take stronger action, and besides, I think we need to draw a stronger contrast with the policies of our opponent. That wouldn't disappoint some members of this council, would it?" Hartwell said, looking directly at Baines.

Baines, who was thrilled with the President's announcement, could only manage a reply of, "No, it wouldn't, Mr. President."

The Joint Chiefs Chairman wasn't mollified. "Mr. President, you know that the armed services have serious reservations about this ban. I know that the bill provides some exceptions for the military, but we need gas powered engines for all of our vehicles. Hybrid engines just don't give our jeeps and half-tracks enough power. You remember how quickly we descended upon Caracas to take out Garcia?" The chairman was referring to the invasion of Venezuela in 2031 to remove that country's president, who had tried to organize an OPEC boycott of the U.S. Garcia had also been accused of providing funding to DOE, a charge that Baines had never believed. "We would never have been able to move with such speed if we'd had hybrid motors powering our vehicles."

Dana M. Stein

"But doesn't the bill exempt all of your armor?" asked the Secretary of State.

"Yes, it does, but we need more than just the armor," the chairman replied. "We know that China has no plans to outfit its newest military vehicles with anything but the most powerful engines. Also, we're worried that with the civilian market for gas-powered cars eliminated, Detroit's ability to maintain the capacity we need will disappear. That's in addition to all the worries about the Big Two losing more market share."

The head of the Environmental Protection Agency jumped in. "I'm tired of hearing concern about the auto industry. After all the bailout money we provided the car companies 25 years ago, they promised they would change their act and develop better, more efficient cars. They did develop products that got better mileage than their previous ones—though that's not saying a whole lot—but their cars hardly went gangbusters in the market. And the Big Two still resisted efforts to reduce our dependence on foreign oil. Setting national goals for reductions of imported oil? Forget about it, thanks to the car companies' opposition. And their promised R&D for a hydrogen car? Never really happened. We wouldn't have had to go into Iraq and Venezuela to protect our oil supplies if the Big Two— or I guess back then, the Big Three—had given enough resources to their engineers to develop the energy-efficient cars that Honda and Toyota did. We wouldn't *still* be at the mercy of OPEC."

D'Alesio replied, "You may be right. But GM and

Ford still have thousands of employees, and it's hard to ignore the fact that their plants are in the swing states."

"All right, all right," an impatient Hartwell said. "I didn't mean to start a full-fledged debate about this. We can discuss the ban if/when it passes. For now, I'll tell leaders on the Hill that we're neutral."

The Joint Chiefs Chairman seemed relieved only a little. "Bret," the President said to the chairman, "we'll work this out, don't worry. Baines, what else should we discuss? Anything in the new Academy report we didn't already know?"

Baines felt that he had thirty seconds to distill what was a major report. "Mr. President, probably the most important recommendation of the report deals with mitigation efforts. They're recommending building many more sea walls along the Atlantic and Gulf Coasts, to protect high-population areas and reduce further exposure to sea-level rise. And they're saying some of the most vulnerable, low-lying areas—such as New Orleans and parts of Miami—should be abandoned, with the population moved inland."

The President drew a deep breath. "How effective have those walls been?"

"Almost all of them have protected areas from sea-level rise. The better ones haven't been breached during storms or hurricanes," Baines said.

"Well, we can't frighten people with proposals to abandon cities. And the budget tab for building hundreds of miles of walls is what, $200 or $300 billion?"

"At least that," Baines replied.

"I'm not about to propose one of the biggest public

works projects six weeks ahead of a presidential election. Baines, make a detailed presentation on this at the first meeting after the election."

With that, the President adjourned the meeting. The Chairman of the Joint Chiefs sat with a puzzled look and then quickly left the room. D'Alesio, who was huddling with the Secretaries of Defense and State, turned to Baines. "Thank you Baines," D'Alesio said. "Your work here is done. We'll need some privacy." With that, Baines quickly left the room and closed the door behind him.

Chapter 5

Margolis got the message early in the morning that there would be a meeting that evening of the Manhattan chapter of DOE at 7 p.m. All of DOE's messages were encrypted, to avoid any interception by the FBI and local authorities. The meeting would be at the usual gathering spot, at the tip of Battery Park.

She had office hours that afternoon, and she tried to disguise her anticipation about the meeting. She was thesis advisor to a few graduate students, and though she found some of their dissertation topics mildly interesting—one student, a contrarian about global warming, was writing about how the current warming mirrored previous warming periods in history—she wasn't very focused, and thought her students could tell.

Instead, her mind was racing ahead to tonight's meeting. She wondered if the head of the Manhattan chapter would

Dana M. Stein

admit that DOE was culpable for the Colorado bombing. She thought it unlikely that DOE was responsible, but she wasn't sure. And what would DOE's next steps be?

Near Washington Square Park she hopped in a cab that slowly crept through rush hour traffic. Her cabbie drove an Atom Car, imports of which had been approved only after years of effort. Even with all of the hybrids and electric cars on the road, the Atom was one of the tiniest cars around, and its small size seemed only to make the cabbie more brazen than most. He darted in and out of traffic, delighting in his ability to weave through tiny spaces in traffic lanes. With all the wild turns the cab driver made, Margolis was pleased to be able to set foot again onto *terra firma*.

She soon saw what had become the new landmarks of the southern tip of Manhattan—walls. The biggest was the wall that surrounded the southern edge of the financial district, erected after heavy rains had flooded everything up to Whitehall Street. Police constantly patrolled the wall, after someone had blown a hole in it a year ago. Margolis had always thought it ironic that with all of the entrepreneurial power of the people on Wall Street, they had to erect a ten-foot concrete barrier to protect them from Mother Nature.

The second wall was more of a fence, designed to keep people out of Battery Park. The city had closed off the park in 2034 after a mother and son were swept into the Hudson River from the park's edge. A nearby boat had fished them out of the water, but the rising water spilled over onto the park's Admiral Dewey walkway so often that city officials felt they had no choice but to close off the park. The fence was an ugly chain-link fence with barbed wire at the top to prevent daredevils from jumping over.

She walked along the fence and gazed through the chain link. Doing so always transported her back to when she was a child. For years, the Saturday ritual for her and her parents was a long, late afternoon walk in Battery Park. She had always enjoyed these walks because the park combined the old and the new. Her first tour of New York had started on a Circle Line ship that docked there. She loved the view of the Freedom Tower as it pierced the sky in full view from the park. When she first saw the Staten Island Ferry, she was frightened by it—it was so big and seemed to move so fast as it glided into the terminal. But when she got to ride on it, she was thrilled, as it seemed to move with such grace and power.

Clinton Castle always intrigued her, almost as an oddity that seemed out of place in the bustling tip of New York City. She loved imagining with her father what it was like to man the huge cannon that had defended Clinton Castle. The castle had originally been built on an island that was connected to Manhattan by a walkway, only to be later connected to land by infill. Margolis thought it ironic that the castle, with water now lapping at its edges, was returning to its original island state.

And of course, there was the view of the Statue of Liberty and Ellis Island. Her father was so proud that his family lineage ran right through that island. Her father never tired of pointing out the name of his grandfather, who had emigrated from Russia in 1903, on the wall at Ellis Island.

As she looked at Battery Park, water hissed as spray came through grates in the pavement. The old Homeland Security building, abandoned several years ago, loomed in the distance at the tip of the park. The only familiar sight from her growing-up years was that of two seagulls, perched atop the pylons that used to mark the causeway to the Circle Line. It gave her a little comfort to think that even if the might of New York City couldn't save Battery Park, at least the seagulls could survive.

Realizing she might be late for the meeting, Margolis quickly walked along the park fence to the Staten Island Ferry building. Once there, she entered a side door that had been left unlocked. She walked down a flight of stairs to the basement, and entered a large storage room that DOE used from time to time as a meeting place.

"Professor Margolis, we were worried you wouldn't make it," said George Bishell, the burly cop who led the Manhattan chapter of DOE. Bishell joined DOE after his son, an Army lieutenant serving overseas, had died from dengue fever, one of the odd tropical illnesses that were now appearing more often.

More than forty people filled the storage room, some sitting on crates, others on half-broken seats that had been discarded from the ferry. They were a varied group, some students, but mostly an assortment of teachers, engineers, architects, and builders. There was no official roster of the chapter's membership, out of fear that a copy might end up with the police. DOE did have a national leader named Rowan—he lived in Arizona or New Mexico, no one was really sure; but all DOE chapters acted independently, so that if DOE members were ever discovered, they could not be linked to the activities of any other chapter. This dated back to when DOE chapters took what were euphemistically called "actions"—cutting the oil pipeline in Alaska, pouring sand in the foundations of new upscale developments, putting barriers in the way of new road construction. Every once in a while, a DOE chapter would do something violent, such as setting fire to the offices of a new car dealership. Perhaps the most spectacular was the toppling of several newly-constructed towers that carried high-power electric transmission lines through coal country.

But if DOE used violent means from time to time, it was understood that damage must be limited to property. No one could ever be hurt or killed. That was clear. That is why everyone at the meeting was perplexed about the recent explosion at the ski lodge in Aspen.

"It just doesn't make sense," Margolis remarked. "It was an appalling action—ten, twelve people killed, including some children? The chapter that did this had to have known that the lodge was operational. Has anyone even been injured in an action before?"

"Never," replied Bishell. "This is the first."

"Could a chapter have wanted to make a statement about the cease-fire," wondered Lucas, a new DOE member who was a computer technician. There had been rumors that some chapters were upset about the cease-fire on actions that DOE's national leadership had declared during the summer. The cease-fire had been announced in advance of Congress' consideration of the ban on combustion engines. DOE's decentralized structure was good for avoiding responsibility for another chapter's actions, but it also meant that chapters had little say in the national leadership's actions.

Margolis replied that if a chapter was voicing its dissent, it certainly could have taken an action that avoided killing people. In addition to the loss of life, this was a terrible embarrassment to DOE. Officials in Washington have been stumbling over each other in their race to denounce DOE the fiercest.

Bishell startled the group with its next comment. "We've been assuming that this was an action, by a DOE chapter. Maybe it wasn't." He flipped open his laptop, found photos of the lodge after the attack, and projected them onto a wall.

"As you can see, this was not your average hill," he said, pointing to the area where the lodge had been located. "It was more like a mountain. I don't know about you, but I can't imagine how a chapter could have done this. Whoever took this action, they detonated several high-powered explosives at the same time, did it in the middle of the night, and left no tracks. A squad of New York's finest couldn't do that. And chapters typically have very few ex-servicemen."

"But wasn't the typical, post-action announcement, with all the right language, sent to the local press?" asked Margolis.

"Yes," Bishell replied. "But there have been enough actions, that the language used in the announcement—that this was done to defend the Earth, that this was a wake-up call about global warming, etc.—is well-enough known."

Members were silent for a minute. "But whether a chapter did this or not, it's clearly shaken up DOE," said Bishell. "And you know what? I'm going to get to meet Rowan. For the first time I can remember, he's summoned the heads of the major chapters to a meeting. I fly out to Albuquerque next week. I'll let you know what happens at our meeting in two weeks. Something is up."

Dana M. Stein

Chapter 6

After he drove away from his farm, the first place Harper stopped at was the Roadside Diner. He must have looked as angry as he felt, since when he walked in the diner, Suzie the waitress said to him, "Harry Harper, I've never seen you look so hot and bothered!" Harper replied that he was heading north and was looking for his regulars. Suzie replied that the only one who was there from his Friday morning group was Bud Jepsen, seated at a table by the corner. Jepsen didn't look as though he wanted to talk to anyone, but when he saw Harper, his face brightened a little.

"Harry, you get the same news I did today?"

"Yessiree, that damn agency said no to my application for relief. Same answer for you?"

"Yep. I can't believe I had much hope that they'd come through. But I thought that with their promises that they'd find something we could grow in this weather, that they'd have the decency to help us out."

"I'd heard that they've run out of money, and though some in Congress are pushing for more money right away, the agency won't be able to spend any more for a couple of months. There's some investigation into whether the agency showed favoritism to the big guys."

"Gee, wouldn't that be a surprise. By the way, we're not the only lucky ones. I heard that everyone in Davis County who'd applied got the same bad news today."

"So Bud, got any ideas as to what to do? You got anything worth a buck that's in the ground now?"

"No, nothing that this drawn-out summer isn't gonna kill."

"I heard that some farmers north of the river—who've been lucky enough to avoid the drought—actually need some hands. If I can't grow it myself, I don't mind finding someone else who could use an experienced tractor hand."

"How far you want to go, Harry?"

"Don't know, but I do have some friends from my days on the board of the co-op. They're north of Ottumwa, so I figure we could start there."

"Well, I'll go with you if you like. Let me get my truck home, meet me at my place, and we're on our way."

Harper took a long look at the people in the diner, said so-long to Suzie and followed Jepsen to his home. Once they were on the road, they headed north on Route 43. They first passed through Bloomfield, which wouldn't have been notable except for the small gatherings in front of homes and shops. Some people had that same hot and bothered look, others simply looked forlorn. "More letters have come in the mail, I guess," said Harper.

It wasn't a long drive to Ottumwa, just twenty miles or so, but Harper didn't drive as if he were in a hurry. It was one of those hot and bright days that would have been rare in September in Iowa in the twenties, but now were commonplace. The air conditioning in Harper's Toyota had given out long ago, so he and Jepsen rolled down the windows and stared out as they drove. What the two of them saw was field-upon-field of brown cornstalks. Some had made it to almost full height, others were shriveled brown stumps. Harper wondered if he could remember what a healthy stalk of corn looked like. Each owner of those fields, he thought, had been proud members of America's breadbasket, just as he and Jepsen had been. Now, having been laid low by forces well beyond their control, they weren't proud of much.

After about thirty minutes, they saw the approach to the bridge that led to Ottumwa. Harper figured that the name Ottumwa had a Native American derivation, and always wondered what it meant. Perhaps it had some relation to the fact that Ottumwa was on the other side of a big river, in this case, the Des Moines River. In any case, he doubted he would find out today.

He had crossed the bridge leading to Ottumwa a thousand times, and a thousand times the view as he approached it had been the same. On the south side was open, flat farmland, on the other was a small city by any city-dweller's reckoning, but a big city in this part of Iowa.

Today, however, the view was different. He and Jepsen

joined a line of cars that led up to the bridge crossing. Each car was being stopped by two men, one in plain clothes, the other one dressed in a dark police uniform. After a brief discussion between each driver and the man in plain clothes, the policeman was waving everyone on. Whatever the reason for the checkpoint, Harper thought, it couldn't be a major issue.

That was until he and Jepsen got their turn to be questioned. As he drove up, he recognized both men. One was his old friend Bobby Hewitt, whom he knew from his days on the co-op board. The other was the Ottumwa town sheriff, a big man whose neck seemed the size of a tree trunk.

Hewitt spoke first. "Well hello, Harry Harper and—Buddy Jepsen?—pleased to make your acquaintance." He paused for a second.

"You're probably wondering what we're doing. We're just asking everyone what their intentions are in Ottumwa and beyond."

Harper was puzzled. "Can't be any hardened criminals or terrorists on the loose in Ottumwa, can there be, Bobby?"

"Well no, Harry. But we've had a different kind of trouble, and we're trying to avoid any repeats."

"What kind of trouble?" Harper asked.

"Well, a month ago some farmers in Northern Missouri got their notices from that agency in Washington, D.C. And three or four of them decided they'd had enough, and would head to north of Ottumwa, where they'd heard things were better. They really aren't that much better up here, you know; we're hurting just like everyone else."

"Doesn't sound like much of a problem to me, Bobby."

"It didn't seem to us at first, either. Initially, these boys—they were all younger, under thirty—said all they wanted to do was find good work. Their farms were now worthless, and all they wanted to do was farm, even as hired hands. And some of the good-hearted people around here gave them work, saying they had a couple of weeks of harvesting."

"The problem was, when those couple of weeks ended, and there was no more work, these boys wouldn't leave. They just stayed in the tents they'd brought with them. And when they were politely asked to leave, they responded by shooting off their hunting rifles. No one was hurt, thank God, but it got pretty ugly."

"So we can't have any more of that. And we know that farmers in Davis and Appanoose Counties got their letters today, and we're suspecting that most of the news was pretty bad."

"I see," said Harper, not really knowing what to say.

"So Harry, I've got to ask you what business you've got north of here."

"We're just going for a ride, to see some friends."

"And who might they be, Harry?"

"Bobby, you and I have known each other a long time, and you know that you won't get any trouble from me. Same goes for Buddy here."

"I'd like to believe you, Harry, I really would, but the sheriff here—well, he's got orders from the Wapello County Commissioners not to let any potential squatter cross this bridge." As to emphasize the point, the sheriff slowly nodded and stared at Harper.

That got Harper's dander up real bad. "I'm not any squatter, and I'm from Iowa, not Missouri," he said, his voice steadily rising. "I wouldn't do that!"

"Harry, you've got to turn around and go back. We're holding up the line here, and, and—there's just no way you can cross that bridge."

His jaw clenched, Harper slowly backed the car up. He wasn't going back, so he took the only option available. He floored his truck and headed west, along Route 34.

Chapter 7

It took more than twenty minutes before Harper could re-gain his composure enough to talk. "Never in my life" he said. "To have an armed sheriff standing guard to deny us entry into another part of the state I've lived in all my life, is unbelievable."

"Think that guy would have shot us if we'd tried to make a run for it over the bridge?" Jepsen asked.

"I wouldn't be surprised if he would have. His reputation is that of a mean son-of-a-bitch."

"Sounds like he'd had his hands full with those Missourians," Jepsen said.

"That still doesn't justify him and Bobby treating us like illegal immigrants trying to sneak across the border from Mexico."

"No doubt about it, Harry. It's just that it sounds like things are tough all over. We knew that our corner of the state was in bad shape, but it sounds like Northern Missouri's been hit hard too."

Harper was calmer now. "I guess you're right, Buddy. Although things are better to the north of us, it doesn't sound like they're that much different. You probably have to go much further north to find farms operating like we remember."

"What I'd heard was that this drought went from southeast to northwest, and heaven help anything that lies in that strip."

"Well, just for the heck of it, do you want to keep on driving until we see some green fields," asked Harper.

"Might as well. It'll be a long time before I want to see the name Ottumwa again."

So Harper and Jepsen continued on their improvised trip. Not wanting to talk anymore about what had just happened, Harper thought he'd change the subject. Both were widowers and had just one son.

"How's that boy of yours?"

"Oh, Jerry? He's fine. He's a lieutenant in the Marines and has been all over the world."

"Where's he been?"

"He was part of the strike force that went into Venezuela a few years back. You may remember back around ten years ago, when things in Saudi Arabia got pretty shaky, he went there just in case the royal family needed our help. Stuck around for a few years to provide some training for the locals, to make sure they didn't have a scare like that again. One of the Saudi royals gave him a sword as a gift—you wouldn't believe all the jewels that sword had. Jerry sent me a picture of him in full uniform, rifle in one hand and that sword in the other, with a big smile on his face."

When Harper didn't respond, Jepsen asked, "How about your son?"

"Oh, Brian? That's a long story," Harper replied.

"Looks like we've got plenty of time," said Jepsen.

Harper hesitated. "It's been a long time since we talked. I can't remember the last time we did, maybe six months ago."

"Fathers and sons can have fights," said Jepsen.

"Not like the one we had earlier this year," answered Harper. "After Brian graduated from high school, he thought he might want to take over the farm when I retired. That was when it still looked like there might be something to take over."

"He studied agriculture at the community college for a while. But when things turned rough, when the drought started to intensify in the early thirties, he started to get angry, real angry."

"Angry at you?" asked Jepsen.

"No, angry at the government. At first he was upset that the Farm Bureau had told us we should stay on the farm, that there was always that tough version of corn that was almost developed. He thought they'd just been lying to us to keep us from panicking."

"Probably was right," Jepsen said.

"Maybe so. I didn't want to think so. You know, the guys at the Bureau had always been straight with us, at least for the most part."

"So then Brian started doing some research about

what the government had done about the warming, starting a few decades ago. That's when he started to get really beside himself. He'd come home from school, and all he'd want to talk about was how the government knew this was coming as far back as forty years ago, and did nothing for too long. He said he just couldn't understand it, that it was a betrayal, especially of his generation."

"I'd try to tell him, look, no one knew that things would happen so fast, that this drought would pick up and turn things upside down. And he'd argue that some people had predicted it, and in any case, there was no excuse for the Feds doing little until about 2012. I think that's when a chunk of Greenland melted, and all the alarm bells really went off."

"So finally, when we both realized he didn't have much of a future if he stayed, he got a hold of himself and started thinking about what he wanted to do. I told him that if he was so mad, maybe he should channel his anger into something productive. He should go and help some of the people who'd been hurt by this crazy weather. So he thought about it, and one day he came home and said that I was right. That he was going to be a firefighter and go out west, where he could be of some use, fighting the wildfires.

"So that's what he's been doing. Last I heard, he's on a special strike force that goes after the fires that move real fast. They call themselves hotshot crews. Dangerous work, but he feels good about it. He used to check in with me from time to time, to let me know that he's all right, but he hasn't called since March, when we had our last falling out."

"Oh, what happened then? If you don't want to talk

Dana M. Stein

about it, that's no problem, you know, I don't want to pry," said Jepsen.

Harper pressed his lips together in silence. After a few moments, he said, "That's okay, it's probably good for me to talk. He said that I should just bail from the farm, that if his mother was still alive, she wouldn't want to see me struggling like I was.

"Well, I'd had enough of his guff, and I thought that was over the top. So I let him have it, and we haven't talked since. I still have his cell phone number, and I've been tempted to call him, but I haven't been able to."

"So how do you feel about what Brian thought?" Jepsen asked gingerly.

"You mean whether he was right to be angry? You know, Buddy, my family's been about as patriotic as you could be. My great-granddad helped liberate France and Belgium in World War II, my dad fought in Iraq, and I was in the National Guard for a long time. I just can't bring myself to think that our leaders intentionally got us into this mess."

"What about what we just went through, at the bridge?"

"I may be goddamm' furious with that sheriff in Ottumwa, but, I don't know, maybe I'm just being stubborn in not wanting to agree with my son."

"So Buddy, if you were in my shoes, what would you think?"

"I don't know. My son and I don't talk much about politics. I'm as proud as any dad could be about him being in the service, but I've got to wonder whether we could have done better. Part of me almost thinks we had it coming."

"Really?" Harper asked with surprise.

"Don't get me wrong, Harry, I don't agree with those people who think that the warming was caused by the state legislature okaying gay marriage, or who think that this was predicted by the Bible. No way. But I think Brian has a point that we could have predicted this mess. I just think our country was stuck in its ways, didn't want to change, until the warming became so clear that we had no choice. And of course once that happened, a lot of damage had already been done. To our farms, to the coastlines, to Miami."

As they headed farther west, through the flatlands of Southern Iowa, the landscape started to change. The fields turned from a dull brown to a light green, and soon Harper and Jepsen started to see signs of farming life. Fields were verdant, with crops that were thriving. They also saw the large wind farms that they'd heard so much about. Wind turbines, several hundred feet tall, towered above the corn and soybeans in the fields.

All of this seemed to lighten the mood, and when they passed a pit beef and barbeque restaurant, they both realized how hungry they were. When Harper pulled into the parking lot, he looked at the map and realized they'd driven quite a distance. "What a difference 100 miles makes," Jepsen said, pointing to the green acres around them.

Chapter 8

After their meal of ribs and chicken, Harper and Jepsen continued their western trek along Route 34. Between the good
food and the break, they felt better. The two shared a feeling
that combined a sense of guarded promise and adventure. At
the pit beef restaurant where they'd eaten, a waitress had told
them that farmers had been able to rent good land in state
parks in the southern part of Iowa. That sounded to them to
be as good an opportunity as any at this point.

After lunch, Harper and Jepsen had pulled out a
state map and scanned Southern Iowa for all of the state
parks. They figured that the farther away they got from
Ottumwa, the better. They found Waubonsie State Park
nestled in the far southwestern corner of the state, and
thought that if any place in Iowa could shelter them
from the troubles that had befallen them, it was there. So

Harper and Jepsen set their sights on a park that, up until then, neither had any knowledge of its existence.

The waitress had scant few details as to what type of farming went on in the parks. "How many farmers were doing this?" they had asked. She didn't know; just that it'd been more than a handful of customers who said they were on their way west. The way they'd talked about it, she said, was almost like they were Moses searching for the Promised Land. Of course, she saw in their eyes that whatever optimism they'd felt was borne out of desperation. "A man who's just lost his farm," she said, "would go looking for any place where he could put a till in the earth."

So on they drove through the Southern Iowa countryside. Harper and Jepsen had both lived in Iowa all their lives, but they'd never seen grapes growing on a hillside until they drove through Clarke County. It turned out that one of the few industries in Iowa that benefited from the warming was wineries. Grapes in Southern Iowa liked the warmer temperatures, and some farmers had converted their farms from corn and soybeans to grapes. Cattle-raising wasn't thriving, but had survived the warming intact, and Harper and Jepsen counted more than a thousand head of cattle along the way.

It was late afternoon when Harper and Jepsen turned south onto Route 275 and then west onto Route 2. Within minutes, they were at Waubonsie State Park, a small, unobtrusive area that was unremarkable except for the hope that it represented to the two men. They turned onto Route 239 and followed the signs to the main campground. They looked for any sign of farming life—a tractor, bale of hay, furrowed rows. They saw no one but a few young campers and a couple who were walking their dog.

Suddenly, Harper and Jepsen felt apprehensive, thinking that maybe they'd been told a tall tale. Still, they didn't give up hope, and they turned around and went north. Maybe they'd missed where they were supposed to go, they thought—the main part of the park was wooded and full of trails. As they headed back to Route 2, they saw a sign for another campground, and headed in its direction. As they got to the campground, they suddenly saw what they'd been looking for—several pickups, and a few hundred yards away, half a dozen men working in what looked to be newly-plowed fields.

As Harper parked his truck, one of the workers put down an old plow and came over to them.

"Welcome, gentlemen," he said. "My name's Lawrence, Paul Lawrence. Where you all from?"

"Out east, in Davis County. I'm Harry, and this is my friend Buddy."

"Pleased to meet you. I guess you'd heard that there was farming to be done out here?"

"More or less," Harper responded.

"I'm going to have to drive back and tell Helen to keep a lid on this," Lawrence said, referring to the waitress from the pit beef restaurant. "But we still have some land that you guys are welcome to do what you can with."

"We'd heard we have to pay someone rent," Jepsen stated. "Each of us has a little bit of money."

Lawrence chuckled. "Rent? For this land? Well, the State of Iowa owns this land, and the good news is that the ranger who's in charge of the park says we can do what we want, provided we don't cause any trouble."

"And the bad news?" asked Harper.

"The bad news is that I'd say we're using farming techniques that are about a hundred years old. No tractors, no machinery, just my mule and a plow that you're welcome to share. Oh, and you fellas will have to cut some brush down from the lots before you can do any farming. We do give you a saw for that," Lawrence said, grinning broadly.

This man has a poor sense of humor, Harper thought to himself. "How much land do we get?"

"Every man gets a one hundred by seventy-five foot plot. Given the modern technology we have to farm with, no one's back has survived to farm more than that."

"And what are you planting in those rows?" asked Jepsen, looking in the direction of Lawrence's plot.

"Corn and soybeans, the usual. Even though we have decent rain out here, fall still runs into November nowadays, so it's not too late to put in a fall crop, if that's what you can call it."

"And where do Iowa's finest go to sell their crops around here?" Harper said with a half-smile.

"Shenandoah has a good auction every week," answered Lawrence.

"That'll do."

"It does okay. It's better than fighting the repo man with pitchforks and knives, as my great-grandfather did during the 1930s," said Lawrence, referring to the last time farmers in the area lost their farms en masse.

"Someplace nearby where we can get tents and camping gear?" said Harper.

"You won't need that. With summer passed, most of the cabins are unrented, and the park ranger lets us stay in them."

"That's awfully good of him."

"You're right; he's top notch. That's why while we've got only a few rules around here, the main one is that if anyone causes trouble—and I mean *any* trouble—then you're outta here. The ranger says his boss in Des Moines doesn't know what he's doing here for us, and he wants to keep it that way."

"Understood. You won't have any trouble from us."

"Sounds good. So why don't you guys put your gear into one of those cabins, and in a couple of hours come down to mine. I'm in the first one. I got some meat from the grocery store today, and I'm happy to share."

After supper, Harper and Jepsen turned in for the night. They each had a small cot with a flimsy mattress, and the bathroom was a small step above an outhouse, but to them, this was plenty. A plaque on the outside of the cabin said that it originally had been built by Camp #607 of the Civilian Conservation Corps in 1935, and Harper wondered if his great-great-uncle Theodore, who'd been a "CCC Boy" for several years, had helped build it. For his uncle Ted, the CCC, with its plentiful food and work and salary of thirty dollars per month, had been the difference between survival and starvation. He'd seen photos of his great uncle with his crewmates, looking tired but content, and standing beside a huge bow-saw they'd used to cut down trees. Harper's grandfather had told him that the CCC and the other programs of the time had helped save the country, and Harper wondered if there'd be anything to save him and all the men like him.

After a while, Harper got tired of thinking. With the encounter at Ottumwa and the uncertain drive west, his body and mind were worn out. Both he and Jepsen enjoyed a deep, peaceful night's rest.

Chapter 9

Margolis knew that with the upcoming changes in her schedule, she needed to meet with her ex, George Hanover, to discuss custody arrangements for their daughter, Alice. Since Hanover was an investment banker on Wall Street, it was difficult to have a productive conversation with him on the phone during the week. When at the office, Hanover usually sounded like a coiled-up spring and was never in a mood to discuss compromise. Instead, when she and Hanover needed to meet to discuss their daughter, they usually met on a Sunday, the one day each week that Hanover had off.

Margolis and Hanover had been married for a rocky five years. They had met when they both were graduate students at the University of Pennsylvania. She was pursuing her doctorate in environmental science and he was an MBA student at Wharton. In addition to his intense brown eyes and black curly hair, she liked the fact that he was one of the few business students who seemed to have a social conscience. He captivated her with his picture of a future in which she would teach the future environmental activists and he would help "green companies" raise the start-up capital they needed for renewable energy and green design projects. Together, they would help turn the tide on global warming and they would love every minute of it.

Half of that vision came true when Margolis accepted a teaching position at NYU. But Hanover, who was fiercely courted by Wall Street firms, decided to go with a traditional investment house that had no green companies among its clients. He would just do that for a couple of years, he told Margolis, so that he could build up a nice nest egg for the family and then go off and start a green venture capital firm.

But the "golden handcuffs," as Margolis liked to call the allure of his big paycheck, kept Hanover in his job indefinitely. Margolis didn't mind the clients Hanover was working for—though many of them included large oil and gas companies—as much as the fact that he was almost never home. During the first two years of their marriage, as Margolis was settling into her teaching work, she didn't care that much; but when Alice came along in year three, things changed. Alice was a colicky baby and her incessant crying tested Margolis's patience. She pleaded with Hanover to spend more time at home, to give her some relief, but one transaction after another kept him at the office, usually until late at night. He would dash home to help put Alice to bed, only to return to the office afterward.

After a couple of years, Margolis became resigned to

the frayed state of their marriage. The closeness they had felt during graduate school days became a distant memory. Their differences—once papered over by their intense love for each other—became more important once things started to fall apart. One of those differences was religion. She was Jewish and he was Lutheran. They both came from fairly secular backgrounds and hadn't thought that they should decide in what faith their children would be raised. But once Alice was born, religion seemed to become more important to both of them. They agreed to celebrate both Christmas and Hanukkah and Easter and Passover. Alice loved lighting candles and putting up lights, so she delighted in having multiple holidays to celebrate.

But when Alice turned seven, old enough to start religious school, Margolis started to chafe at their religious compromise. After all, she thought, she provided 90% of the parenting, so why shouldn't Alice get to know her religion some more? But Hanover wouldn't agree. If Alice was going to go to Hebrew school, he said, Alice should also go to Sunday school at the uptown church his grandfather once attended. Going to two religious schools was an impossibility, of course, and the result was an impasse.

Despite the challenges, Margolis was resolved to keep their marriage together as long as possible. Hanover was a good dad when he was home and his salary supported living in a nice brownstone and family vacations to exotic locations. Margolis delighted in visiting Costa Rica's rain forest, climbing Machu Picchu in Peru, and surveying the animals of the Galapagos.

Her resolve ended, however, the day she discovered

his affair. It was a brief dalliance that Hanover swore had ended. But it was with his secretary Laurie, whom Margolis had invited over for dinner many times, and Margolis just couldn't abide his infidelity. She also couldn't get the image of the two of them together out of her head.

So when she confronted Hanover with the evidence—a receipt for roses that had not been delivered to her—she also told him the marriage was over. He didn't fight her too much, but what he did fight her over was her insistence that he get only one weekend a month with Alice after their divorce. He had changed barely ten diapers; never taken her to school; didn't know what she liked to eat; so how could he take care of her? He countered that he, with his paycheck, funded the diapers, the food, and the private schooling. When she didn't budge, he stunned Margolis by threatening to tell the family court judge of Margolis's involvement with DOE. She finally relented to regular weekend visitation rights, and she never forgave Hanover.

So given their bad blood on visitation rights, they always clashed when one or the other tried to change the schedule, even if for one week. This time was no different. They met at a donut shop that Sunday morning at 9 a.m.—Alice, an eight-year-old who loved to sleep in, was still at Margolis's apartment, with a babysitter in the unlikely event Alice woke up—and they immediately started sniping at each other.

"I need to have you look after Alice all of next week, I'm going to be away," said Margolis.

"Where you going?"

"Not that you really need to know, but I'm going to visit my mother."

"For a whole week?"

"Thanks for asking how she's doing, by the way. I'll also be visiting a new solar array—remember that, solar energy? Something you once thought about supporting as a venture capitalist?"

"You're not visiting your underground friends out west who have a penchant for violence, are you?"

"You jerk, you still can't resist bringing them up."

"They're criminals and should be doing time."

"Aside from the merits of what they do, I find it a little ironic for someone who cheated on his wife with his secretary—wasn't that a fireable offense at your firm?—to question the actions of others."

"It's apples and oranges, Emma, and you know that. And you know I felt terrible about the affair."

"Only after you got caught."

"Okay, no sense in rehashing the past. I can keep Alice that week and get someone to look after her each afternoon."

"Fine, thanks, I suppose."

"How is your mother doing?"

"Mind still sharp, body not holding up too well. We still talk all the time."

"Send her my regards."

"I'll do that."

With that, the two said so long. As they left and she walked away, she remembered how Hanover had been a good man, at least until work became a demon that completely overwhelmed him.

Chapter 10

As Margolis returned to her apartment on Bleecker Street, she felt relieved that the meeting with Hanover was over. She also was glad that she had scheduled a fun activity with Alice: a visit to one of their favorite locations in New York—Central Park.

Margolis was a bit of a celebrity with Alice's third grade classmates. No other parent was a professor, let alone someone who was regularly quoted in the press on climate change. Alice was always on the lookout for ways to involve Margolis in her class' studies. It was partly because she loved showing off her mom, but also because she secretly thought that her mom and her teacher, Mr. Montford, would be a perfect match. When Mr. Montford announced that they would be studying New York wildlife the following week, Alice leapt to her feet to volunteer her mother for a trip to Central Park. Mr. Montford

Dana M. Stein

smiled broadly and obliged Alice's request. More proof, Alice thought, that he had a crush on her mom.

So at 11 a.m., Margolis picked up her daughter, and together they rode the subway to Central Park. Alice had thought it'd be fun if she and her classmates came to the outing dressed as one of the creatures found in Central Park, and Alice had chosen to look like the Eastern Tiger Swallowtail. All that week, Margolis and she had painted pieces of tag board to look like the wings of the butterfly, complete with the detailed yellow-and-black finery that marked the swallowtail. At the last minute, Alice decided the outfit needed something more, so Margolis found some sequins to add. Margolis carried Alice's elaborate costume with her on the way to the park.

As they rode the subway, Alice chatted cheerfully about how her classmate Howard was going to be a turtle, Betsy a rabbit, and Jonathan a green frog. She was sure she would have the prettiest costume. Her mom looked at Alice and thought that if her parenting had been successful at nothing else, at least she was raising a girl who loved nature.

At the 81st Street exit, Margolis and Alice got off the subway, walked up to street level, and crossed into Central Park. Once in the park, Alice took off. Margolis, who yelled to Alice to wait for her, could barely keep up. As Alice got winded, she finally slowed down, but not without commenting on how slow she thought her mom was. Margolis started to brag about how fast she could run when she was young, but then thought better of it.

The class was to meet at Turtle Pond. Margolis and Alice walked past the Great Lawn, which was filled with families and couples enjoying the sunny and warm weather. Sights of parents and kids picnicking and playing frisbee always gave Margolis a twinge of regret about her divorce. They would never be the perfect family, though Margolis knew that families rarely were.

As she frequently did when Margolis strayed into a melancholy thought, Alice got her attention. Alice had started to clamor for a dog, and once Margolis had found out that the apartment building would permit small dogs, Alice offered commentary on the small canines they would encounter. Today, it was the dachshund they saw chasing a ball across the grass. "A dachshund would do just fine," Alice pronounced. Margolis sighed and smiled, partly because a dog was the last thing she wanted at this point, and also because she had grown up with a big, loveable golden retriever and couldn't quite envision having a dog the size of a big cat.

Once they got to Turtle Pond, they met up with Alice's classmates, their parents, and Mr. Montford. The children quickly put on their wildlife regalia—Alice the butterfly, with her beautiful, bedazzled wings; Howard the turtle, with his clunky cardboard box that simulated a pond slider's shell; Jonathan the frog, with his green felt for skin and flippers for toes; Betsy the rabbit, with grey felt for fur and a big cotton ball for a tail; and several others. Alice voiced approval of all the costumes except that worn by the student dressed as an eastern red bat. Alice hated bats.

Margolis came equipped for her presentation with many picture books. She figured she could skip the discussion of bugs and other invertebrates, but she knew the class would love to hear about the turtles, frogs, and mammals. As they sat at Turtle Pond, she pointed out the Snapping Turtles, Florida Cooters, and Eastern Painted Turtles that were swimming about. Howard was disappointed that they saw no frogs, but Margolis said not to worry, there were still plenty of frogs in Central Park—though in more tropical areas, some frog species were vanishing because of rising temperatures.

She then turned to the birds. She pointed out the pairs of stately mallards swimming in the pond, the brown females swimming just a little behind the green-headed males. Margolis discussed how the Canadian geese would migrate south but not just yet; with a longer autumn, they headed south two weeks later than they did ten years ago. She told the class how the Turkey Vulture and Red-tailed Hawk lorded over the skies of Central Park, and how the park was full of varieties of wrens, warblers, and sparrows.

At this point, she noted a frown on Alice's face. *Aha,* she realized, *she hadn't yet discussed butterflies.* So she proceeded to discuss the different kinds of swallowtails in the park. She told the class that the number of butterflies had dropped in the park and no one knew why. Margolis described how the monarch butterfly was famous for its long migrations. Alice seemed much happier now.

After Margolis finished her presentation, the students thanked her and wandered off with their parents. Alice asked Mr. Montford if he would walk with them, but he politely declined. Alice was very disappointed, but she and her mom wandered to their favorite spots in the park—the sheep meadow and the nature sanctuary.

Margolis loved the quiet of the meadow. When they got to the southern edge of the park, Alice fretted when she saw the horse-drawn carriages, but Margolis told her not to worry, most of the horses were well-taken care of.

Having walked more than a couple of miles by this point, the two stopped for an Italian ice and sat quietly on a bench on Central Park South, watching the stream of people and cars pass by. Though she had spent many years in Manhattan, Margolis never tired of people-watching. She and her daughter would play a game in which they guessed who among the crowd-goers was famous and to what adventure they were headed. Today, Alice spied a woman with willowy blond hair and commented that she must be the new Princess of Scotland, off to see the castle in Central Park. She would claim the castle as her own and rule over all the butterflies in the park.

It was now late in the afternoon, and Margolis noted that her daughter looked weary from the afternoon's adventure. Margolis and Alice rarely went anywhere except by subway or on foot, but today Margolis hailed a cab. After she gave directions to the cab driver, she turned and looked at Alice. She had already fallen asleep.

Dana M. Stein

Chapter 11

Baines rarely had any weekend days off, especially since the Presidential election remained tight. However, on the first Saturday in October, he was able to block the entire day off, first to do some volunteer work and then to have lunch with his sister, Abigail.

A year earlier, Baines had joined the board of a local non-profit called D.C. Green. The group's mission centered on preparing low-income residents to become entrepreneurs in renewable energy and conservation. Its executive director was Hector Ruiz, a charismatic middle-aged man who had grown up on the streets of Southeast D.C. and who had a passion for greening communities. He connected well with young men who needed a job and with local businessmen whose arms he twisted for contributions to D.C. Green. Knowledge of finances, however, was not Ruiz's strong suit, and Baines had already bailed

D.C. Green out of a financial hole by finding a low-interest loan that saved the day at the last minute.

D.C. Green's many graduates included several sole proprietors who operated out of a pickup truck. Some were installers of solar film, which had replaced traditional solar panels in the 2020s. As the cost of solar film declined, D.C. Green's graduates found many customers in the high-income neighborhoods of Northwest Washington who wanted to show off their environmental sensibilities with arrays of solar film on their homes.

Other program graduates had become one-man shops for retrofitting homes to improve energy conservation. They could do everything from installing energy-efficient lightbulbs to blowing insulation into walls to installing solar-powered water heaters. They had become so proficient at improving energy conservation that several promised they'd reduce power use by one-third or homeowners would get their money back.

Still others had found a niche in the booming field of biofuels. Ruiz liked to refer to these graduates as his "farm boys," since they had taken over many of the vacant lots in D.C. and started growing switchgrass, which helped power the ethanol plant on the edge of town. If there was any silver lining to the rising temperatures on the East Coast, it was that switchgrass could easily be grown in Mid-Atlantic States. As wood chips became another economical input in the production of biofuels, his farm boys pooled their resources and bought a wood chipper. After every storm, they would go door to door in leafy neighborhoods and haul away fallen tree limbs for practically no charge. They would then convert the limbs to wood-chips and sell the product to the ethanol plant's fuel supplier for a tidy sum.

One of D.C. Green's training programs involved sending out crews of trainees to the homes of senior citizens to install the energy conservation basics—light bulbs, low-flow showerheads, water aerators for the kitchen and bathroom sinks, insulation wraps for water heaters. This package of items cost only $100, but could save homeowners twenty-five dollars per month on their utility bills. Baines was not very handy—his tool supply at home consisted of only a hammer and a screwdriver—but he could screw in light bulbs and install a showerhead, and most of all he enjoyed getting out of the White House to do a hands-on project.

So on this Saturday, he volunteered to go out with D.C. Green's crew to a senior high-rise in Southwest D.C. The crew nominated Baines to be the team leader, which meant he was the one who at each apartment, introduced the team and described the items they would install. Their goal was to complete work at five apartments that morning.

At the first apartment the team visited, Baines fumbled a bit, not being quite familiar with the script, but by the time they reached the third apartment, he had the presentation down pat. "Hello, Mrs. Saunders, I'd like to introduce the members of D.C. Green's Energy Savers team—Carlos, Mike, and Luwanda. We're here to help you save money on your energy bill, at absolutely no cost to you." After explaining the different items in their arsenal, the team would then methodically replace the existing light bulbs with new LED bulbs and install the aerators and showerheads.

Baines had never liked heights, but dutifully climbed the team's rickety ladder to reach the light fixtures in each apartment's living room. He was pleased that he didn't embarrass himself by dropping any bulbs, but he made a mental note to mention at the next board meeting that D.C. Green should spring for some new ladders. He also was amazed at the number of old, inefficient incandescent light bulbs he found; Congress had phased them out of production years ago, but seniors hadn't wanted to throw them away. Some habits die hard, Baines thought.

Most of the seniors knew that D.C. Green would be coming and thanked the team for their work. A couple of the residents, however, seemed to be in poor shape. One senior could only mumble as she stared at the television; at first Baines and the team didn't know what to do, but when she seemed to wave them in, they proceeded with their work and left quickly. Another senior was sweating profusely—she couldn't afford the cost of turning on the air conditioning, even on hot and muggy days—and she had lost her blood pressure medication and been told she couldn't get a refill for a month. Baines told the team they should make an appointment for her at the health clinic down the street, and he'd make sure she got her refill.

At their last apartment, the team found a woman, Layla Watts, who seemed very happy to have visitors. She chatted up the team as they made the rounds in her apartment installing light bulbs. After they'd installed the water aerator in the kitchen sink, Layla invited them to stay for tea

Dana M. Stein

and cookies. Baines, nervous about making his train to Baltimore to meet his sister, politely said he had to leave.

Still, she insisted, and Baines—never one to disappoint a woman who reminded him of his grandmother—agreed to stay for a few minutes. When Layla asked each of the team members what they did for a living, Baines demurred, but team member Mike said that Baines was a big shot who worked for the President. Immediately afterward, Layla's demeanor changed. Her lip began to tremble and she started to weep.

"Oh, sir, you've got to help me. My son, daughter-in-law, and their daughter are down by the Anacostia in that camp. It's terrible."

Baines was a bit unnerved by his having to quickly switch into official work mode. Still, he wanted to hear what she was talking about.

"What exactly is the situation, Miss Layla?"

"Conditions are awful down there. I just spoke with my son the other day. The sewage treatment plant broke down, and sewage overflowed right next to the camp. The smell was horrible, and my grandbaby got sick."

"I'm so very sorry. Do you know if she's better?"

"She is, but Mr. Baines you've got to go down there and fix the conditions. It's not right. They did nothing wrong except live where the Anacostia rose because of the warming."

"All right, Miss Layla. I'll do that."

"You promise me you'll go visit?"

"I promise, yes ma'am."

Her demeanor improved a little. "Well alright then, you all finish your cookies and then I'll let you head back home."

Chapter 12

After finishing his work with D.C. Green, Baines got ready for his meeting with his sister Abigail.

Abigail and he, separated in age by only two years, had always had something of a contentious relationship. Abigail had brains before she had looks, and Baines had always been just a little jealous of his sister's smarts. When she and he overlapped in high school for two years, he had ignored her, as most older brothers would a younger sister, but he still felt guilty for not helping her when she was mercilessly bullied by other girls for being a nerd. The bullying stopped in her junior year when she suddenly blossomed into a pretty brunette who could command respect from the boys as well as the teachers.

Her anger toward Baines for shunning her in school had slowly dissipated over the years, but not her sympathy for the underdog that her unhappy first years in high school had created. That sympathy had meant that she and her brother had taken divergent paths in their careers as lawyers. Baines had taken the conventional route, working in a blue-chip law firm in Washington, D.C. before joining the National Security Council several years later. Abigail, on the other hand, had worked in the Legal Aid Bureau in Baltimore before joining a public interest firm that represented plaintiffs in civil rights and environmental justice cases.

In late September, Abigail had called her brother, concerned about their dad and his status as a homeless person camped out on the National Mall. They'd agreed to meet for lunch that Saturday, so a little after noon that day, Baines hailed a cab for the ride over to Union Station. He was tired after his volunteer work with D.C. Green and didn't look forward to his lunch meeting. The cab ride didn't soothe his grumpy nature as he was riding in an old clunker of a car that had long been banned. At first Baines thought he should report the driver and took down the cab's number, but then thought better of it and crumpled up his note.

He hopped out of the cab and walked through Union Station. With so few non-work hours, Baines rarely had time to shop for anything, so he enjoyed window shopping in the station's stores during the few minutes he had before the train departed. He loved looking in the shop that sold toy trains, especially the old Lionel models. It was fun to look at the old, boxy train models as they chugged around the circle-eights that were set up in the store. Trains from that period seemed very antique compared to the sleek, high-powered trains that were the custom now.

Soon after, Baines got on the 12:30 p.m. Northeast

Express, whose first stop was Baltimore. It was one of the newer magnetic levitation versions, which meant that it took only ten minutes to make the trip from Washington to Baltimore. The trip on the "mag-lev" was so quick that Baines once had dozed off and awakened thirty minutes later in Trenton.

Soon after the train pulled out of the station, it was on its way. The magnets that propelled it were so strong that the scenery passed by in a blur. The train was remarkably quiet, since its wheels hovered a few inches above the track unless it was entering or leaving a station. Baines had always marveled at the train's technology and the aerodynamic design of the cars. From his seat in the top part of the double-decker train car, he had a commanding view of the landscape. The corridor on which the train ran had very little countryside left. Instead, it was populated by small cities and suburban sprawl and the dense traffic that was ubiquitous in Maryland.

When the train slowed down for the approach to Baltimore's Penn Station, Baines was reminded that despite all the changes in train technology, one thing had not changed. Most tracks still took trains through the poorer parts of cities, and Baltimore was no exception. The Northeast Express passed through neighborhoods that seemed to teem with tenements. With the swelling of Baltimore's displaced population, poor neighborhoods had gotten more crowded and poorer. Baltimore was home to some of America's finest hospitals and universities, but prosperity's advance remained stalled outside most of the city's older, low-income neighborhoods.

As the train approached the tunnel into Penn Station, it slowed down and descended onto the tracks, and made the same clickety-clack noise that trains had made for two centuries. As the train slowed to a stop at 12:45 p.m., Baines bounded off and headed up the steps from the track to the station. He had always loved to walk through Penn Station. It had the same marble floors, old-style lamps, and musty smell that train aficionados like Baines loved.

He then boarded Baltimore's subway, which took him to the harbor. Baltimore's subway was plain but efficient, though Baltimoreans didn't pack onto the subway as Washingtonians did theirs. He always felt like a sardine when riding Washington's subway, but in Baltimore, the subway car was half-empty. A few stops later, Baines exited the subway and walked toward Baltimore's harbor, where the seafood restaurant that he and Abigail were to meet at was located.

As Baines caught his first glimpse of Baltimore's harbor, he thought about the times when as a teenager he had helped his father with his crabbing. His father always needed an extra hand to maneuver the boat while he pulled up the crab pots that he had set in the Chesapeake Bay, so Baines would go along. Perhaps it was the early hour that they headed out or the smell of the boat, but regardless, Baines was a most reluctant helper. Baines also didn't like the fact that it was his job to assemble all of the necessary items the night before. This included the crab pots or traps, tongs, bushel basket, measuring ruler, crabbing license, their breakfast, and the chicken necks his father used as bait.

When his father pulled a trap from the water and found a crab within, it also was Baines's job to shake the crab into a bushel basket. He would then measure the crab from point-to-point to make sure it was of legal size—Maryland had a strict minimum size of crabs that could be caught—and he'd also check the crab's apron or underbelly to see if it was male or female. Females were protected by state law and had to be tossed back. Baines would also throw back crabs that were too small. He knew that some crabbers circumvented these restrictions designed to replenish the crab population, but his father was very precise in his observance of the rules.

During the springs and summers that he helped his father, he would sit quietly and do his tasks, but it was obvious to his father that Baines disliked the work. After a while, his father stopped asking him to go along and found a neighbor's son who took more interest. Baines now regretted that he hadn't used these outings as a way to get to know his father better.

Another result of his crabbing experience was Baines's strong dislike of seafood. Baines's father often grumbled that no self-respecting Marylander could dislike seafood, especially crabs, but Baines didn't like their taste, especially with all of the Old Bay and other spices that locals would put on steamed crabs. What also didn't help was that one of Baines's other tasks was to hold the lid on the pot of crabs as they were being steamed. That led to nightmares in which Baines dreamt that relatives of the steamed crabs would seek their revenge, snapping their claws over him as he lay in bed. After several instances of

Dana M. Stein

helping send dozens of crabs to their steamed fate, Baines made a point of being absent from the house when crabs were being readied for cooking.

He found Abigail sitting at a table, focused on a thick legal document that she had brought with her.

"Hello, brother," she said. "I hope you don't mind meeting me here—I know a seafood-house is not your favorite venue—but I thought we could admire the view that used to be."

"For you, sister dear, anything." Baines replied.

Abigail was referring to the three-meter-high, two-meter-thick wall that now encircled the harbor. That had replaced the smaller one, which hadn't held the waters that Hurricane Alberta had stirred up in 2035. After churning north through the Chesapeake Bay, Alberta had turned inland into the Baltimore harbor. With winds exceeding one hundred miles per hour, it had leveled most structures within two hundred feet of the harbor. The harbor had experienced a building boom during the preceding decades, with new $2 million condominiums rising each year on the harbor's perimeter. Most of those buildings had been seriously damaged, if not destroyed, by Alberta.

The tall cranes that unloaded thousands of tons of cargo each year at the city's port also fell victim to the hurricane. Not built to sustain winds of Alberta's magnitude, their crossbars came unlocked as Alberta entered the harbor, so that the cranes looked like flippers on pinball machines. Then, the cranes' uprights started to sway back and forth, taking on the appearance of gangly monsters with unsure footing. One by one, the cranes—one of the few remaining reminders of Baltimore's rich blue-collar heritage—came crashing down, sometimes on top of each other, making a horrible racket.

Perhaps most tragic for Baltimore's heritage, Alberta had also wreaked serious damage on Fort McHenry. What the British bombardment of 1814 hadn't achieved, was accomplished by the hurricane's stout winds. The breaching of the harbor's seawall seriously eroded the point on which the fort stood, so that water now lapped up to the wall of the fort. The fort and its old cannon now looked to be defending the city not from any foreign invader, but from Mother Nature herself.

The view that Abigail referred to was one of a devastated shoreline that was slowly being rebuilt. Baltimore's harbor had been a major tourist attraction for decades, but now featured only a few shops, restaurants, and condominiums that had dared to be rebuilt on a shoreline that had moved a few yards inland. There was a gaping hole in the harbor where the USS *Constellation* had once stood. Alberta had torn apart the ship, which was famous for having fought the slave trade on the high seas in the nineteenth century, timber by timber.

"I spoke with Dad the other day; he seems okay," Abigail said matter-of-factly.

"You know, I do check in on him every day," Baines replied, somewhat testily.

"Yes, I know you're being a good son. How much longer does he plan to stay there?"

"Lord knows. He claims he has no plans to move. But

even with the warming, winter in D.C. is no cakewalk. I've repeatedly asked him to move in with me, but to no avail."

"I've seen your place, and one would have to have a high tolerance for clutter to live with you."

"You try working my hours. Besides, my apartment can't be any worse than the Mall. Have you been there? One of the subtle hints that the park police drop for them to leave is not emptying the trash cans anymore. The tent area on the Mall has started to smell a little ripe."

"If that's the worst that the park police do to them, that would be okay. I hear the regular rumors that Dad and his friends are going to be rounded up and relocated to a flophouse in D.C."

"I hear those rumors too."

"Anything you can do about them?"

"Not much. I make phone calls to the park police headquarters, and they tell me that despite the complaints from the tourists about the appearance of the Mall, nothing will happen before the election. The President doesn't want to come across as harsh on the homeless."

"Ahh, your 'President.' What a guy. Wouldn't want to do anything that's reminiscent of the attack on the jobless vets that MacArthur led in 1932, at least before the people have voted in November."

"That's him. As you know, I'm not terribly fond of the guy."

"And neither are we. You know, Michael, I wanted to meet with you to discuss Dad, but also to tell you something else."

"The suspense is killing me."

"You're not going to like this. You know that lawsuit that Stewart & Simon decided not to take? My firm's going to take it."

"What, you mean that suit representing disgruntled farmers against the executive branch for failure to act against climate change? Abby, you've got to be kidding!" Baines was starting to get agitated.

"No, I'm not. Assuming we can get past the sovereign immunity issues, you know that we've got a good case. Your predecessors in the White House did next to nothing for almost fifteen years, despite all the mounting evidence that the warming was real."

"Well, good luck in being able to convince a jury that Congress would have approved climate change legislation in those days, even if the President had recommended something. But that's not why I'm mad. What I'm angry about is that this is going to be very embarrassing for me. You have to know that."

"I do," replied Abigail. "But this case is too important to let go. Look, at least I told Dad he couldn't join as a plaintiff."

"What?" Baines's face was beet red. "Dad wanted to join the case? That ingrate!"

"I didn't prompt him. It just came up in our discussion that the firm was going to take the case."

"Well, I hope that your firm is going to be hiring, because once it gets out that my sister is suing my employer, I may be looking for a new job."

Baines sat glumly at the table and picked at his food. "Couldn't you at least wait until after the election to take the case? A couple more months wouldn't hurt."

"The other partners and I discussed this, but we decided that it was important to file the case before the election and while Congress is considering the gas-engine ban."

"How much in damages are you going to be asking?"

"Oh, given that the government in its wisdom has wiped out some of the most productive farmland in history, we figure in the range of $250 billion. Given the way the federal deficit is going these days, you won't even notice if you actually have to pay it out."

"Just remember, Abby, I've been doing everything I can on climate change. The wheels of government just happen to grind slowly."

"The polar bears are gone, except for the zoos; the Arctic ice cap doesn't exist in summertime anymore; some Pacific islands have disappeared; and the wheels of government still grind slowly? With statements like that, you should be glad I won't depose you!"

"Good luck with your case, sister dear. It's been swell catching up."

With that, Baines got up and left the restaurant. Within forty-five minutes, he was back at his office in the Old Executive Office Building, looking at the archives on government decisions on climate change. Baines thought about the legal arguments to come, about which files were discoverable and which ones were subject to executive privilege. All pointless discussions, he thought, as the imperatives of climate change grew greater every month.

Chapter 13

One week after his arrival at Waubonsie, Harper was in a reflective mood. One thing was certain—he had never felt so tired in his entire life. Lawrence had promised backward farming conditions, and Waubonsie did not disappoint.

First, the only things that had ever grown in his farming plot were grass, brush, and trees. The Waubonsie eight—as the group had come to call themselves—shared a small rototiller that did not like tough soil or rocks, both of which were in great supply in Harper's plot. The rototiller's noise and racket was much greater than the tilling it did. On top of that, Harper felt like his shoulders were being pulled apart when he used the machine. Harper's soil was about the rockiest he'd ever seen, and he built small piles of rocks along the edges with what he collected from the soil. With all the rocks lying along his plot, he thought that someone could easily have mistaken it as the foundation of a building from a time long ago.

After he was done with tilling, Harper faced the challenge of getting several big tree stumps out of the soil. For that, he needed Harvey. Harvey was Lawrence's old mule and the only farm animal in the park. Pulling tree stumps was a poor way to make an introduction with Harvey, but after several tries, Harper finally coaxed him to pull out the stumps.

Harper generally had no use for mules, since they reminded him of all the chores he had to do when he was a child. And the feeling was mutual, as Harper, eager to make a go of things at Waubonsie, didn't give Harvey any break. After Harper built up the soil with the few items he had at his disposal—some manure, but mostly leaves and mulch—he hitched Harvey up to the plow and started making his rows. As a young boy, he'd heard lots of stories about how farming was so much harder for his ancestors, and while he had doubted the stories when he heard them, one row of plowing now erased all doubts. After each row, Harper would take a break and sit under the shade trees that were plentiful in Waubonsie. Harvey would give him a look that said he'd make a run for it if he could, but every time Harper got up from his break, Harvey would put his head down and plow ahead.

After a week of back-breaking effort, Harper and Harvey had gotten the plot ready for planting. By this time, Harper felt a sort of kinship with Harvey—both of them had been dealt a raw hand by the warming. Harper had had his fill of travails, and Harvey probably had to give up a quiet life on Lawrence's farm to help the motley crew in Waubonsie. Harry and Harvey were easy names to mix up, and after a while Harper didn't mind it when the other farmers got him mixed up with the mule. A mule is certainly stronger than he was, Harper thought, though he had worked as hard as any mule could since he got to Waubonsie.

Harper then went and put his corn and soybean seed down by hand. After he stooped and covered each of the rows—work that did not ease his aching back—he stopped and looked at his plot. It may have been a pitiful sight compared with his farm in its heyday, but he was proud of his work of carving a small field out of almost nothing. All he needed now was some rain, something that the drought in Southeastern Iowa had erased almost all memory of.

Soon enough, though, rain did come, and his corn and soybean seeds started to sprout. The field was speckled with small shoots of green, and as the days passed and his corn stalks grew, Harper's hope grew with them. Even though he was a squatter in a state park with few farming tools to speak of, he now had something to look forward to. Every day, he would get out of bed and rush out and check on the plot, like a proud papa admiring his children.

The members of the Waubonsie eight were a quiet group. They would share a midday meal and talk about their crops, but at night they repaired to their cabins to ease their aches and pains and mull over what had come of them. It was too hard to think about the future, and no one really talked about it. Harper gleaned that some of the farmers were family men, but most everyone was reluctant to talk about their children, for it reminded them of the tragic turn their lives had taken. Some would find the courage to call their family only after wandering off onto one of the winding trails. There, in the cover of darkness that hid their embarrassment, they would talk with their children and let them know that yes, they were all right.

Within a couple of weeks, the Waubonsie eight had grown to twelve. A few more poor souls from Southeastern Iowa had shown up at the park. As long as they accepted Lawrence's rule of no trouble, the group made room for them. There was still enough open land that could be tilled. They had run out of empty cabins, so when Lawrence asked for volunteers to share their space, Harper and Jepsen willingly obliged. Harper recognized one of the farmers as from his own county, a man named Sisco, and said to him, "You look like you need a good night's rest, take my bed and I'll use my sleeping bag."

Since Lawrence had been good to him, Harper decided that the way to return the favor was by taking Sisco under his wing. Also, he had the advantage of having a working understanding with Harvey, which not all of the farmers could claim. So Harvey let Harper hitch him up for his fellow farmer from Davis County. Sisco was impressed with the way he got Harvey to work, though Harper claimed that Harvey always kept one eye on the row ahead of him and one eye on him.

One day, Harper got the nerve up to ask Sisco for any news from back east. He said there wasn't much; that several farmers in the area had gotten letters from Washington the same day that Harper did. Sisco was slower to respond to the bad news than Harper was, in part because he had some livestock and a Labrador retriever. He was able to sell his few head of cattle to a neighbor, but he was reluctant to part with his dog, which had stuck with him through thick and thin. He still remembered the look his dog gave Sisco when he dropped him off with the friend who had agreed to take him in.

Sisco said that he had initially thought about going north, but that he had heard about what had happened to Harper in Ottumwa. That got Harper's attention real fast.

"You heard 'bout that?" he asked.

"Well yes, Harry, we heard about it at the diner. Someone was in the line in back of you at the bridge, and when he came to the crossing, he asked the sheriff what had happened, and the sheriff told him."

Harper muttered something unmentionable under his breath about the sheriff. He tried to rationalize the news by saying that the encounter at Ottumwa was bound to get out sooner or later, but for the rest of the day he couldn't focus.

At night, Harper would take walks through the park and admire the night sky. With winter coming, Orion was making its appearance in a low arc. Harper recalled how his son Brian loved looking at the moon and the planets with his small telescope. Though never much of a hunter himself, Harper enjoyed telling stories about Orion the hunter and how it was chasing its prey through the night sky. It was when Orion would come into view that Harper realized how much he missed his son.

One night, just after Orion had started its nightly march, he pulled out his cell phone. It was still well charged since he hadn't used it much since he'd come to Waubonsie. He started to call Brian, then hung up. *How would he be able to tell his son all that had happened,* he wondered. Then he opened up the phone and started dialing again. He shivered a little, a combination of the chilly air and his nerves. He got Brian's voice mail, and left a long, rambling message describing the odyssey that had led him to Waubonsie. At the end, he paused and told him that he missed him and he loved him. He then walked slowly back to his cabin. Orion was now marching higher into the sky.

Chapter 14

It was a cool, crisp October day in Washington, and as Margolis disembarked from her train at Union Station, she decided to walk to Capitol Hill. Today was the final day of testimony before the Senate Environmental and Public Works Committee on the bill to ban gas-combustion engines, and she had been called as a witness. The House of Representatives had already passed the bill by a clear margin, but in the Senate, the predicted vote was much closer. Even from afar, as she approached the Hart Senate Office Building, she could tell that it was a scene of bedlam.

Margolis had always been impressed by the immaculate care that Congress took of the lawns and flower beds leading up to the Capitol and office buildings. Today, there was little green space to be seen, as protesters on both sides of the gas-engine bill had assembled in large and vocal numbers. Environmentalists were out in force

Dana M. Stein

and were chanting, "Heed the warning, end the warming!" School children were holding up pictures of a sad-looking polar bear with words underneath that said, "How many more will follow him into oblivion?" Large numbers of auto workers were also present, holding pictures of shuttered auto plants and demanding, "Save Our Jobs!" Then there were the religious groups, most of whose members sat and prayed below signs that said that climate change was God's punishment for the government's policy on gays or its overseas military interventions.

Margolis pushed through the scrum of protesters and press and made her way to the cavernous committee hearing room. She registered with the committee's clerk and took her assigned seat, knowing that it would be some time before she was called.

By now, the testimony on both sides had become quite familiar and predictable. Proponents of the bill warned that average world temperatures would soon be perilously close to a tipping point, beyond which the climate changes already manifested would become even more dramatic. Though Margolis couldn't disagree with their analysis, she thought they sounded too much like apostles of doom and gloom.

Opponents warned of the bill's impact on an already-beleaguered auto industry that, despite major improvements in fuel efficiency and battery-cell technology, still claimed the need to manufacture some cars that were powered entirely by gas engines. Some Japanese car companies had already shifted most of their models away from gas engines—both Toyota and Nissan sold cars powered exclusively by batteries; but cars and trucks sold in the U.S. were on average larger with more horsepower. This, according to the representatives of General Motors and Ford, necessitated defeat of the bill, or at least more study of its impact.

The Administration had taken a position of studious neutrality on the legislation, promising only to review it if and when it was presented to the President. This, it was thought, reflected the position of an ever-cautious president who did not want to rock the boat before Election Day. However, think tanks normally associated with the Pentagon testified in opposition to the legislation, warning in dire terms that unless the armed forces were excluded entirely from the bill, U.S. security would be irreparably harmed by its passage.

As the hearings stretched into the afternoon, Margolis's mind wandered. She thought about her recent trip to New Mexico, where she had visited the huge solar panel array near Albuquerque. The array covered 2,000 square miles of desert and contained thousands of photovoltaic cells, and produced 100 gigawatts of electricity. The array stored energy using a novel compressed-air energy system, which pumped air into abandoned mines and underground caverns. When released, the compressed air generated electricity by turning a turbine.

The solar array was part of the alternative energy program approved by Congress in 2015. The program funded construction of a large new infrastructure to support solar and wind power. The solar plants and wind farms were to be located in barren parts of the Southwest U.S., where the sun and wind were plentiful. But because these stretches were far away from urban or suburban centers that needed electricity, huge new transmission lines had to be constructed, necessitating a major outlay of public funds.

Sponsors of the plan had argued that to combat global warming and reduce dependence on foreign oil, the U.S. needed to commit to a $500 billion program that underwrote the infrastructure costs of alternative energy. Under the plan, the U.S. would be producing 2,500 gigawatts of clean energy and importing practically no foreign oil by 2060. Most in Congress agreed with the plan, arguing that it cost less than U.S. subsidies to the oil, gas, and nuclear industries. A determined minority of representatives from oil-producing states, however, fought the plan and blocked it in the Senate. As a result, the plan that passed was a much-watered down version of the original proposal. Congress authorized $200 billion over a thirty-year period, a significant investment, but much less than necessary to achieve independence from foreign oil.

When Margolis visited the New Mexico solar array, damage to the high-voltage transmission line that connected several solar plants to the Phoenix area had been repaired. The trans-Alaska oil pipeline had been damaged by a shotgun blast earlier that year, and in retaliation, saboteurs had blown up part of the solar transmission line. Margolis was impressed with the size and efficiency of the New Mexico plant, which had been one of the first large solar plants to come on line. A few more like the New Mexico plant had been built in Arizona and California, generating an aggregate of 300 gigawatts of electricity, but Margolis knew that many more solar plants would be needed to make a real dent in global warming emissions.

While out in New Mexico, Margolis had taken a side trip to visit her mother, who lived in an assisted living facility in Albuquerque. Margolis and she were very close— they talked nearly every day, and after Margolis's father had died in 2030, they had gotten even closer. Margolis's mother had hoped to be able to stay in New York, close to her only daughter, but her bad allergies made it impossible to stay in an urban environment. Rising temperatures had doubled the pollen content in cities like New York and Philadelphia during the spring and summer. So she reluctantly moved out west, where the clearer air alleviated the discomfort caused by her respiratory ailments.

This was the first time Margolis had visited her mother since she had helped her relocate to Albuquerque. It had been hard for Margolis to leave her mother at the facility, but she was pleased now to find that her mother was comfortable and relatively happy. After initially warehousing the flood of aging baby boomers in large assisted living facilities and nursing homes, companies had switched to constructing small, cottage-like settings for seniors, which residents liked much more. Margolis especially enjoyed catching her mother up on the latest developments in New York political and literary circles. She was very practiced at deflecting the usual questions from her mother about her social life and whether she planned to marry again. The hardest part of the visit was seeing her mother weep when Margolis showed her pictures of Alice, whom her mother had not seen in almost a year.

Dana M. Stein

Finally, at about 3 p.m., Margolis got her turn to testify. As a consultant on the new report of the National Academy of Sciences, she was asked to explain its findings. Since the report had been front page news, she was concise in her review of it. She knew that a couple of the undecided committee members were from Midwest states that were home to both farmers and factories that made parts for Detroit cars. So she focused some of her testimony on the expected impact of intensified warming on farming. She said that the drought that had hit parts of Missouri, Iowa, and Nebraska would expand in reach. While some northern states had experienced an increase in farm productivity as a result of higher temperatures, that situation would not last forever. The Academy's report, she noted, said that an increase of another degree in average temperatures would wipe out agricultural gains in Minnesota and Wisconsin.

Once her testimony ended, the committee started to pepper her with questions. She had predicted the queries about the Academy's methodology, which she handled with ease. What she had not expected were the more blustery questions from the Senators.

"If Detroit stopped making gas combustion engines tomorrow, would global warming stop?" asked one of the bill's opponents, Senator Redfern.

"Well, that's highly unlikely, Senator. Even with this bill, we will continue to add carbon dioxide to the atmosphere, and temperatures are likely to go up, at least somewhat."

Redfern replied, "If this bill will not stop the warming,

then why should we cripple the auto industry and cause it to stop making cars that U.S. consumers want to buy?"

"Senator, gas-powered engines still emit a substantial amount of carbon dioxide, and this bill would help mitigate any further warming that—" Before she had a chance to finish, Senator Redfern announced that he was finished with the witness.

Senator Morgan then asked for a point of clarification. "Professor Margolis, I'm a bit confused. You say the Academy warns of the supposed peril of temperatures increasing by more than two degrees, yet you said earlier in your testimony that temperatures had already increased by two degrees."

"Senator, my apologies if I wasn't clear. I had said that average worldwide temperatures had increased by two degrees Fahrenheit. The Academy is referring to two degrees Centigrade, which is a larger change."

When several in the audience chuckled, Morgan's face turned a deep crimson. "Professor, are you paid for your consulting work with the Academy?"

"Yes, Senator, I am."

"Do your earnings constitute a significant part of your salary?"

"I wouldn't say significant, but given the pay of college professors, it isn't insignificant."

"Does your status as a paid consultant influence your opinions?"

"Not at all, Senator. My testimony today is very similar to the information I present in my college courses."

"And speaking of your college students, do you ever encourage them to engage in civil disobedience?"

"Excuse me, Senator?"

"Civil disobedience! Such as protests on campus or here in Washington, D.C."

"Senator, I don't encourage my students, nor do I discourage them. I do encourage them to participate in the political process as full, engaged citizens."

"And do you know of anyone else who has engaged in civil disobedience, or the destruction of property?"

"Senator, I fail to see how these questions pertain to the subject matter of my testimony."

"Professor, they go to any bias you may have in your testimony. Do you know of others who have engaged in civil disobedience, or have you attended any meetings with people who may have?"

"Senator, I believe my political associations or beliefs are not the proper subject of any inquiry here." The crowd murmured, and an exasperated Margolis looked for some relief to the committee chairman, who finally joined in by telling Senator Morgan that his time had expired, and that the witness was excused.

Baines, who had sat as an observer during the hearing, intercepted Margolis as she left the hearing room. "Professor, we should talk. I'm Michael Baines, member of the NSC with responsibility for climate change issues."

"Oh yes, I've heard of you, Mr. Baines. Mostly positive."

"Well, thank you."

"What do we need to talk about?"

"Oh, the usual—the future of the planet, how many of

us will survive global warming, etc. Perhaps a little more mundane than that."

Margolis smiled at Baines's attempt at humor. "I'll be back in a few days for the international treaty discussions. I assume you'll be representing the administration at the conference?"

"Yes. Perhaps we can meet up then?"

"Certainly. Though based on the questions from that inquisition masquerading as a Senate panel, I don't know if you want to be seen with me."

"I'll take my chances. Besides, talking with you will be a welcome break from the chatter of earnest U.N. functionaries at the conference."

She smiled again. "Well, you have a date then."

Chapter 15

Harper got along pretty well with most of the farmers at Waubonsie. He had been friends with Jepsen for a long time, and they and Sisco had managed to stay on good terms despite sharing tight quarters. Harper was one of the older members of the group and didn't mind sharing his knowledge of the quirks of growing corn and soybeans with the younger farmers.

However, there were two members of the group who were rather non-communicative. One was a fellow from South Central Iowa who appeared to have been so traumatized by the loss of his farm that he preferred to speak very little. He worked hard during the day at his plot, but said practically nothing during the group dinners and didn't come out of his cabin during the evening.

The other was a farmer from outside of Council Bluffs who had a bit of a temper. His name was Beasley, and he growled at farmers he didn't like and yelled at Harvey if the mule wasn't fully cooperative. The way he treated Harvey got under Harper's skin, for he respected the mule for his work and in general didn't like to see animals abused.

One night, Beasley got drunk and started a fistfight with his cabin mate, accusing him of stealing his straight-edge razor. The next morning, Lawrence and others, including Harper, stopped Beasley as he left his cabin to tell him that he'd just slept his last night in Waubonsie. Between this eviction notice and a bad hangover, things didn't sit too well with Beasley.

At first he was all bravado, saying that he'd been evicted from his farm a few weeks ago and wasn't about to be evicted again. He'd just had a little disagreement with his cabin mate, he said, and no one should give two hoots about that. When it became clear that the group was serious, Beasley broke down and cried. He said he'd lost everything, his farm, his wife, and his self-respect. Please give him another chance, he begged. "Can't do that," Lawrence insisted. "We can't have anyone getting the police out here or causing trouble for the ranger. You knew what the rules were." Finally, Beasley stormed off, saying he would be back, like it or not.

That left everyone a bit unsettled, but Lawrence told everyone not to worry about it, that Beasley was all bluster. When the park ranger heard what had happened, he came running to Lawrence and told him that they were putting his job in jeopardy. The Iowa Park Service wouldn't like it if they found out that the group was cutting down trees to clear land, he said, and they certainly wouldn't like that he was hosting farmers who got drunk and into fistfights. "Not to worry," Lawrence assured the ranger. "Beasley was gone, wasn't coming back, and no one else would cause any problems."

Harper was not too concerned, having grown up with a father prone to drinking too much whiskey, especially when the farming news wasn't good. As a child, Harper could always measure how bad a drought was by how drunk his father got in the evening. So Harper went about his business and, as his corn and soybeans continued to grow, he figured it was time for him to visit Shenandoah. He knew from the other farmers how the town's auction functioned, but he thought that with the time growing nearer when he'd be taking his crop to town, he should go and visit.

He found Shenandoah to be not very different from the towns he'd grown up with in Southeastern Iowa. People were pretty friendly, and given the drop in corn production throughout much of the state, the prices that were offered at auction were pretty good, about ten dollars per bushel. The corn auction happened every other Wednesday, and the soybean auction took place on alternating Fridays.

On the short ride back from Shenandoah, Harper was focused on the mechanics of getting his crop to town. The way his corn was growing, he might have to make several trips with his pickup to haul it. Given that this was his first corn crop in a couple of years, how to transport it to Shenandoah was a problem he didn't mind at all. Of course, picking his corn by hand was an exercise that he didn't relish very much.

But when Harper turned onto Route 2 and approached the entrance to the park, he was startled by what he saw.

Black smoke hovered over the northern section, the part that was being farmed. He thought that perhaps someone had set a fire to clear away thick brush, and that the fire had gotten out of control. He floored his truck and quickly got to the campground.

What he saw was a scene of complete chaos. All of the farmers were screaming and yelling, their faces red with anger. Then he saw why. Beasley had returned, determined to get his vengeance. He and several of his pals had stormed into the park with their pickups, shouting and cursing. At first they drove through several plots, tearing them up as they went. Harper's plot was one of the unlucky ones. Then they got out of their pickups and proceeded to destroy Lawrence's plow. Two of the farmers tried to stop them, but they were no match for Beasley's gang, who were armed with shovels and baseball bats.

As Harper got closer, he could see that Beasley was completely drunk. While generally angry at everyone, Beasley's temper was focused on Lawrence, and he and a pal had turned to giving Lawrence a bad beating. He, Jepsen, and Sisco managed to pull the two off Lawrence, screaming that they should get the hell out of there.

For a moment it seemed that Beasley might take their advice. He hopped back into his pickup and swerved across a field toward the road. But then he did a U-turn, and headed back toward the plot that a farmer had been plowing with Harvey. Beasley got out of his truck and began chasing after Harvey, aiming to beat him with a shovel. He was swearing that he was going to teach that "good-for-nothing mule" a lesson. As Beasley pursued

Harvey, he swung his shovel at the mule's hindquarters every few steps. The first several times, he swung so wildly that he missed and fell down.

Harvey, whose eyes were wide open in fright, desperately tried to avoid Beasley and his shovel. But the poor mule couldn't run very fast, and Beasley was charging like a madman. It wasn't long before Beasley won the footrace. As he raised his shovel again, it looked like he was going to whack Harvey over the head. Just as Beasley started to bring the shovel down, Harper pulled out the .38 that he kept in the small of his back and fired a shot over their heads. That froze Beasley in his tracks and got everybody's attention.

Beasley swore at Harper that he'd kill him, and he then called to his crew to get Harper. Harper dashed back to his pickup and zoomed onto Route 2. He thought that Beasley's gang would be less likely to pursue him if he left Iowa, so he headed west on Route 2 and soon crossed the Mississippi River into Nebraska.

When he had driven about ten miles, and with no sign of any pursuers, Harper pulled off onto a local road and into the parking lot of a convenience store. Just to be safe, he pulled around to the back of the lot and parked face forward, just in case he'd have to make a getaway. He called Jepsen, who was relieved to hear from him. Jepsen told him that Beasley and crew had taken off after him, but that he suspected they wouldn't go far, given their state of inebriation.

"Do you think they'll return to Waubonsie?" asked Harper.

"I doubt it," Jepsen replied. Just to be safe, they had

called the police. "You know, Harry, you saved our skins back here. Lord knows what other kind of damage they were going to do. Lawrence took a bad beating, but he'll be okay. By the way, he says to thank you, as your shot probably saved Harvey."

"I didn't hit anyone, did I?" Harper asked sheepishly.

"Nothing but a tree in the park, most likely." Still, you probably should stay out of the area for a little while. Knowing Beasley, someone in his gang will probably report you as having tried to kill them, those sonofabitches."

"Don't worry, I have no plans of returning. What are you all going to do?"

"I don't know," said Jepsen. "I've had about enough adventure as I can take, so I'm probably going to hitch a ride with one of the men who's going back east. What I do when I get home, I don't know. Lawrence and some of the guys want to try to stay, but the park ranger is about as livid as he can be. He says that thanks to us, he's going to lose his job. So I doubt he'll let anyone stay."

"That's a shame. We weren't giving anyone any trouble. That idiot Beasley had to go ruin it all for everyone."

"So where you going to go, Harry?" asked Jepsen.

"I dunno. I may just drive until I get some inspiration. You know this truck of mine gets 750 miles to the fill-up, and I still have a little room on my credit cards."

"Your son ever call you back?"

"He did, after a while. We didn't talk long, as he was fighting a big fire in Yellowstone Park."

"You know anyone else west of the Mississippi that you could cool your heels with?"

"Not a soul, Buddy, at least no one I've spoken to in years. But you know, I've always wanted to see Las Vegas," Harper gamely offered.

"Harry Harper, I could take you in a game of poker with my eyes closed. Don't waste your money."

"I guess I'll just head west then."

"You call me when you get to wherever you're going. I'll let you know if there's any word of anyone looking for you, that is, in case you'd like to come back."

"Buddy, you've been a good friend. I don't know when I'll be back, but until then, you take good care."

Chapter 16

In mid-October, environmental ministers from around the world gathered in Washington to consider new international protocols on limiting greenhouse gas emissions, or GHG. The first international agreement on climate change had been the Kyoto protocol in 1997, which was followed by the Johannesburg accord in 2011, in which countries agreed to reduce GHG emissions by 30%. The U.S. Senate had failed to ratify the Johannesburg accord by two votes, leaving the U.S. out of the treaty and giving America a huge black eye in world opinion.

Johannesburg had been followed by the Toronto treaty in 2025, under which countries agreed to reduce GHG by 50%. The Senate did ratify the Toronto treaty two years later, and the U.S. was making substantial progress toward reducing its emissions. Congress had approved a cap-and-trade program for power plant emissions and had mandated mileage stan-

Dana M. Stein

dards of fifty miles per gallon for cars by 2038. The problem was that while the U.S., Japan, and the European Union were making significant efforts to comply with the Toronto treaty, China, India, Russia, and other countries were in serious non-compliance with the treaty's obligations.

As a result, countries gathered that fall at the World Bank to consider ways to improve compliance with the treaty, as well as to lay the groundwork for a follow-on agreement. There wasn't much hope of substantial progress at the talks, given the pending U.S. presidential election, but almost all signatories to the Toronto treaty had agreed to start discussions.

As the international delegates gathered in Washington, protesters started to pour in as well. Environmental groups had mobilized tens of thousands of demonstrators, and since the talks were at the World Bank, groups protesting conditions in developing countries turned out as well. Global warming had caused drought in parts of South America and Africa, and rising sea levels had exacerbated the grinding poverty of Bangladesh. Though AIDS was finally under control in the developing world, some countries in Africa and parts of India had virtually been wiped out by the disease. The resurgence of malaria and dengue fever, largely caused by warming temperatures, had also turned into a major problem. The World Bank had poured resources into fighting these new plagues, but some organizations felt that it wasn't enough.

Protest organizers assembled a huge rally for the first day of the talks. By 10 a.m., demonstrators had gathered at the intersection of Pennsylvania Avenue and 19th Street. They started marching down Pennsylvania Avenue, with the goal of turning onto 18th Street and stopping just in front of the World Bank. However, battalions of riot control police met them and refused to let them turn onto 18th Street. The riot police had a very menacing look, dressed in black, wearing dark helmets, and carrying truncheons at their sides. Many people held their breath as the sea of protesters surged toward the police, but the demonstrators stopped just short of the police line. There were some tense moments as protesters hurled eggs and tomatoes at the police, who responded by lobbing some tear gas canisters, but the protest organizers had agreed that they would not instigate any fights. Some of the organizers still had wounds from the beating they took when a protest in New York City got out of hand, and they were reluctant to experience that again. So after some pushing and shoving, the demonstrators agreed to pull back and hold their rally on Pennsylvania Avenue.

Meanwhile, at the conference, it became apparent early on that India and China would defend their record by accusing developed countries of breaking their treaty obligations. The Johannesburg and Toronto accords had promised significant aid to developing countries to assist them in reducing GHG emissions. India's environmental minister accused the U.S. and E.U. of providing insufficient technology and direct financial assistance. The head of the U.S. Environmental Protection Agency quickly disputed that, arguing that the U.S. had provided billions of dollars in aid. The Indian minister questioned the EPA Administrator's assessment, and the back-and-forth continued throughout much of the first day.

Dana M. Stein

Baines was attending the conference as a U.S. representative, but by early afternoon the bickering had grown tedious. He text-messaged Margolis, who was also at the conference, to say that now was as good a time as any to meet. He suggested that they meet at a coffee shop in Georgetown, sufficiently far away from the conference so that their meeting would probably go unnoticed. She agreed to meet him at 2 p.m.

What should have been a leisurely fifteen-minute walk for Baines turned into a more extensive trek. The smell of tear gas still hung in the air, and streets and sidewalks still had police barricades. Baines had to detour north through Farragut Square, and as he turned into H Street, he was surprised to see some broken storefront windows. Angry demonstrators, it seemed, had vented their frustration by throwing rocks through the windows of banks and brokerage houses. *Above everything else—stalled global warming talks, the latest bad news on wildfires out west—that'll be the lead story on the evening news*, Baines thought.

Baines arrived a few minutes late. At first he couldn't locate Margolis, as the coffee shop was packed with veterans of the morning protest who were chatting in animated fashion. He found Margolis seated in a corner booth, and after Baines sat down, they both fidgeted nervously. Margolis opened the conversation.

"So, Mr. Baines, don't you have more important things to do than to meet with professors with dubious standing before the U.S. Senate?"

"Only if they happen to be the most roguish," Baines replied.

"Then apparently I qualify, at least according to the climate change skeptics on that Senate committee. Boy, and to think they invited me to testify."

"Redfern and Morgan have reputations for being loose cannons. I wouldn't take it too personally."

"I don't, but I do think they did a good imitation of Tail Gunner Joe McCarthy. Asking me about my political associations, for crying out loud? Oh well, at least my students loved it—the grilling I got improved my cred with many of them."

"I bet it did. NYU has always been good for generating agitators—I should know, I went to law school there."

"You did? Somehow, I don't see you as being the agitator type."

"Oh, I traipsed through Washington Square Park with protesters on more than one occasion. Can't really remember what I was protesting at the time."

"You seem to have quickly settled down. Not too many ex-NYU protesters can say they have a seat on the National Security Council."

"If you heard some of the discussions at the NSC on climate change, you'd realize I'm not as orthodox as you might think."

"Well, counselor, what led you to want to meet with me?"

"You know, the President would like to sign the gas engine ban, if the bill makes it out of the Senate."

"And that has to do with me—how?"

"The only way he's going to sign it is if it doesn't hurt

Dana M. Stein

his re-election chances. And that means no more actions by your friends with the deer-like name."

Margolis put down her cappuccino and stared directly at Baines. "What makes you think I would have any influence over them?"

"I'm not saying that I know this to be a fact, but your reputation as a DOE sympathizer does precede you, almost as much as your expertise on global warming science."

"You know that even if that was true, I'd never acknowledge it."

"All right, all right. Let's just say hypothetically, if you did know any of the key leaders of DOE, it would be very helpful to tell them to cool it, at least through November. If anything remotely like the Colorado bombing happens again, the President will run away from that bill as fast as he can."

"What makes you think DOE was behind the bombing," Margolis asked.

"It was the type of target that DOE has gone after in the past."

"Yes, but with two major exceptions. First, it killed people. DOE has never done that. Second, it required capabilities that DOE does not have—assuming, hypothetically, that I know what capabilities DOE does have. A paramilitary force would have to have done it."

"And why would someone try to frame DOE?"

"Baines, you're not as smart as I thought you were. How many people don't want the President to sign that bill? And I'm not talking just about the car companies. You saw how those defense industry toadies were spitting nails during their testimony. They made it sound like we would be giving away our nuclear secrets to the Russians or the Chinese if that bill passed."

"This is the first I've heard about someone else doing the dirty deed and trying to finger DOE."

"Don't you read the blogosphere? Oh, I forget, you're too busy for that," said Margolis with a half-smirk. "Okay, how enthusiastic are the Joint Chiefs about the bill?"

"Not very."

"And after the stunts that the CIA pulled in Venezuela in the early thirties, do you think anything is beyond them? Despite all the rules about those involved in black ops not being able to do any domestic actions, do you think they're sticklers for the law?"

"I still can't believe it's true."

"Besides, Baines, I have it on good authority that the DOE folks have called for a big rally right before the election, at which they're going to go public and renounce all violence entirely. Given all of that, I doubt that, even if I'm wrong about the Colorado bombing—which I'm not—that your President has anything to worry about."

"I hope to God that you're right. You know if the Republican gets in, then we're all finished. He won't do anything about global warming until the Potomac rises up and starts lapping at the front door of the White House."

"Well how about this? After the election, let's meet again and compare notes. Besides, it's been a long time since someone as important as you has invited me to have coffee with him."

For the first time during the whole conversation, Baines managed a smile. "You're on."

Chapter 17

Baines hadn't forgotten his promise to Layla Watts to see the Anacostia camp, and he figured this afternoon would be as good a time as any to follow through. As he emerged from the coffee shop and said good-bye to Margolis, he noticed the skies were threatening. He quickly bought an umbrella and hailed a cab.

When he told the cabbie where he was headed, the driver gave him a quizzical look.

"I've never had someone from this part of town ask for a ride to the Anacostia."

"Well, it's a first for me too."

As they drove east through D.C., the skies got darker. "Looks like we're in for a good bit of rain," the driver offered.

After a twenty minute drive, they finally arrived at the camp. As Baines got out of the cab, he was surprised by what he saw. Row upon row of cinder-block homes was what made up the camp. Sheets and shirts flapped in the wind from clothes lines. The camp had one main road through it and dirt roads connected the camp's subdivisions. All in all, Baines thought, it was the type of development he'd seen a lot of in South America's poorer cities.

He finally located the home of Miss Layla's son and daughter-in-law. It was in the second row of homes located adjacent to the river. He knocked on the half-torn screen door. When no one answered, he knocked harder. A dog around the corner started to bark. Finally, a young woman with a scarf over her hair came to the door.

"Hello, ma'am. I'm Michael Baines. I spoke with your husband about coming by."

"Oh yes, Henry had said you'd stop by. He's still at work, but come on in. My name is Mary, and this is my daughter, Becca."

Rebecca was a shy three-year-old who hid behind her mother's skirt. She had big brown eyes that stared plaintively out from a round, innocent face.

"Mind if I have a quick look around?" asked Baines. "I promised your mother-in-law I'd make sure your house was in decent shape."

"Be my guest," answered Mary. "Whether this counts as decent shape, I don't know."

Baines quickly understood Mary's embarrassment. The house was made up of four rooms, spartanly-furnished. The floor consisted of plywood with some tattered rugs thrown on top. The sofa, cabinets, and lamps all looked like they'd been pulled from a room in an abandoned hotel. The living room doubled as the couple's bedroom.

Dana M. Stein

"Your air conditioner work alright?" asked Baines.

"It doesn't keep the muggies out most summer days," Mary said, referring to D.C.'s humidity.

"This past summer was a tough one, I know. Can we sit and talk a bit? I told Miss Layla I'd call her after I visited."

"That's fine. She can be a very persistent woman, I know. Have a seat, and I'll get you some iced tea."

"That'd be fine."

As Baines sat down at the kitchen table, he noticed that it'd started to rain. The raindrops came down hard on the home's tin roof.

"When it rains hard at night, the racket makes it difficult to sleep," said Mary as she brought in the iced tea. "At least the roof keeps the water out, that's about the only good thing I can say about this place."

Suddenly Baines's phone beeped. He opened it and saw its message: "Flash flood warning, D.C. metro area."

Flash floods had become all too common in recent years and low-lying areas in D.C. had been hit hard.

As he looked through the kitchen window, he saw that a small stream had started to form outside of Mary's house. It looked like it was headed straight for the river.

"Do you have anything outside that you need to secure—any flower pots or toys?" asked Baines.

"A couple of things. I'll be right back."

Within a minute, Mary rushed back into the house. "Mr. Baines, the water outside is moving very fast!"

Baines looked at the two-foot stream that had formed outside the kitchen. It was moving swiftly and carrying clothes and debris with it. The rain was coming down in a deluge.

"How many homes are right next to the river?" he asked.

"Three or four. One of them has kids at home, just like me."

Baines dashed out the door. The stream had widened to three feet and was shin-deep. On any other occasion, Baines would have avoided ruining his shoes and suit if at all possible. But he had to cross the stream to get to the houses by the river, so he dashed straight through.

He ran to the first house and knocked. He heard a television on inside, but no one answered. He used his shoulder to break through the flimsy lock and found a teenage girl talking on the phone as a younger brother did his homework. Both seemed oblivious to what was happening outside.

"You've got to get out of here! The whole area is flooding!"

Baines didn't wait for them to respond. He grabbed the girl and boy and pulled them from the house. "Go toward higher ground!" he yelled, pointing in the direction of a small hill.

He then ran to the second house. No one answered and there was no sound from inside, so he ran to the next. By this point, the stream had broadened into a small river and Baines had to fight to make it across and to avoid the tires, wood and toys that the water was carrying.

At the third house, Baines found a woman frantically pulling canned goods and clothes into a suitcase. "There's no time for that," Baines yelled. "You've got to get out now! Follow me!"

The woman, sensing the danger that Baines was conveying, quickly complied. But as they ran from her house, she told him that there was an elderly man in the house next door.

After Baines had helped the woman to safety, he ran toward the fourth house. He broke in through the door and searched the house for its elderly occupant. He finally found him, terrified and hiding from the storm in a closet. The man wasn't an invalid, but he had trouble walking.

"Can you swim?" asked Baines.

The man just shook his heard. "Sir, I'm going to get you to safety. You just hold on to me as tight as you can."

As they stepped off the porch, Baines waded into the flood waters with the elderly man on his back. At first Baines thought they'd be okay, but he quickly realized they were being pulled toward the river by the waist-deep water. Baines wasn't strong enough to fight the current and for a few seconds he thought they'd both end up in the Anacostia. But he saw a tree up ahead, and he yelled to the man to hold on. He knew he would have one chance to grab a tree limb that was above his head. As he leapt for the branch, he grabbed it but the man tumbled off his back. In one motion, he grabbed the man's shirt and pulled him back.

Not sure if the branch would hold them both, Baines shimmied his way to the tree trunk, where they stayed for the next twenty minutes, holding on for dear life. The man was trembling and getting very tired, but he held on. Baines would not let him go.

When the water finally receded and the paramedics reached Baines, they immediately put the man into the ambulance and gave him oxygen. Baines stayed with him for a few minutes, waiting for the man's trembling to stop. When it did, Baines got out of the ambulance and looked toward the river. All four homes had been swept to the river's edge and the middle two had actually gone in. Baines hoped that no one had been in the second house.

After a minute, a wave of weariness came over him and he crumpled to the ground. He turned around and the ambulance was gone. Baines realized he never had learned the man's name.

Dana M. Stein

Chapter 18

Baines woke up early the next morning. His experience at the Anacostia camp had been unnerving, and his dream that night had been a strange and disturbing one. The dream had started off pleasantly enough; he dreamt that he and Margolis were taking a long, afternoon stroll up Connecticut Avenue toward the apartment she had recently rented. Suddenly, though, they heard a hue and cry as they passed the Washington Zoo. People ran screaming from the zoo, with the children in a particular state of panic. Baines couldn't understand what they were hollering about, but as he saw a tiger running toward Connecticut Avenue, he realized that many of the zoo's animals had escaped. Some had leapt over their fences, others had slammed their bodies so forcefully against their cages that the metal bars had broken open. They were angry, and they were venting their rage by pursuing any person in sight.

Baines told Margolis to run toward her apartment, but as she started to dash away, she tripped over a man who had fallen in the panic. Baines turned to help her, but as he did, he saw a hippopotamus barreling down the street toward him. At first he believed he could outrun the creature, but it was quicker than he thought possible. Foaming at the mouth and snorting loudly, the hippo terrified Baines. He started running down Connecticut Avenue. He darted in and out of traffic and ran through alleys, but every time he thought he was safe, the animal would emerge in hot pursuit. Finally, as Baines got close to his apartment, he was sure the hippo was gone. But as he got to the door, he fumbled with his keys, and the hippo found him yet again. It started to charge him, and Baines imagined the horror of being slammed against the door by the huge, squat animal. He finally found his key, and as he opened the door he woke up.

As he got dressed, Baines recalled the movie *The Birds* and thought that Hitchcock would have been proud of his nightmarish creativity. He just hoped the dream wasn't an omen of how his day would go. When he got to his office in the bowels of the Old Executive Office Building, though, he decided that maybe the dream was a portent after all. An investigator from the FBI, heavy-set and with short legs, was there to greet him. *Maybe the hippo was meant to symbolize this visitor from the FBI,* Baines thought.

Baines knew that FBI investigators had their jobs to do, but they still gave him the willies. They wore three-piece suits, even in the middle of summer, asked endless questions, and poked their nose in all aspects of your busi-

Dana M. Stein

ness. When the FBI investigated Baines for his security check for his White House job, FBI staff had dropped in at his old law firm and roamed around NYU's law school, asking whether Baines had ever used mind-altering drugs, ever participated in radical environmental groups, or said anything particularly seditious about the U.S. government. Baines had been very happy when the investigation for his background check was complete.

So when the FBI investigator showed up at his office doorstep, Baines's mood turned sour. You couldn't tell him to come back another time, since that would only make him suspicious. Fortunately, though, Baines had a good idea of why the FBI wanted to talk to him, and he knew that he was in the clear. The lead story in that morning's *Washington Post* was about an investigation into whether the insurance industry had bribed key members of the Senate Banking Committee to approve a bail-out of the industry.

The hurricane that hit Southeast Florida in 2032 had caused big losses for several of the nation's largest insurers. In response, these insurers had announced that they would no longer insure any coastline property in the three states most vulnerable to rising sea levels—Florida, Louisiana, and Maryland. The legislatures in each of those states replied by saying, not so fast—and required each insurer to continue offering casualty and property insurance to coastline property owners, even if at extremely high rates.

Insurers protested, and their legal challenge to the three states' actions was winding its way to the Supreme Court when Hurricane Alberta hit Maryland. That hurricane pushed the two largest insurers into bankruptcy, and several others teetered on the brink of collapse. The insurance industry then played its last card by calling on every last "chit" it had on Capitol Hill, and got a bill introduced that bailed out the industry. Prospects looked good for the bill's passage—nobody in Congress wanted the federal government or the states to have to serve as insurers of last resort—but insurance executives, naturally being cautious people, wanted to cover their bases. The *Post* claimed that they had rounded up large campaign contributions on the eve of the Senate committee's decision on the bill, leading to a lopsided, favorable vote.

Baines had recently dated the committee chairman's chief of staff, Robin Murphy, so Baines guessed that that was the reason for the FBI's social call. Sure enough, he was right. The investigator wanted to know about his relationship with Murphy and whether she had ever discussed "financial incentives" from the industry, as the investigator put it. Baines answered that he had heard not a word about any such incentives, and that his relationship with Murphy had been short-lived. The relationship had been steamy, tumultuous, and brief—too brief, as far as Baines was concerned— so there was little Baines wanted to say about it. Still, the investigator persisted. How long had they dated? Where would they meet? Baines thought all of this was none of the FBI's business, and he finally told the investigator off.

FBI investigators weren't used to being told to be quiet, and this one was no different. His next question caught Baines off guard. "So, I assume you knew that Robin Murphy was married?" Baines hadn't known, and he muttered something to that effect. The investigator smiled a wry smile—he

Dana M. Stein

had just delivered Baines's comeuppance, and he figured that if Murphy hadn't shared with Baines that she was married, she probably hadn't shared any other secrets.

"Thank you for your time, Mr. Baines. If there are any more questions, I'll be in touch. Here's my card in case you think of anything else." With that, the investigator was gone. Baines quickly closed the door, sat in his chair and stewed. So *that* was the reason why Murphy never wanted to go to the usual Washington, D.C. gathering spots. *That* was the reason she always wanted them to go to his apartment. Knowing that she was married eased his disappointment about being dumped a little, but he wished it hadn't been an investigator in a polyester suit who'd delivered the news.

Baines stared out the tiny basement window in his office. He knew he had to refocus his thoughts quickly as he was going to a meeting with D'Alesio, and he had no idea how it would turn out. He stood up, took a deep breath, and closed the door to his office.

He walked over to the West Wing and entered D'Alesio's office. "You know we only have half an hour to the Council meeting, so you'll have to talk fast," D'Alesio said.

"Will do, Rick." He'd known D'Alesio long enough, and D'Alesio had enough respect for Baines's smarts, that he was one of the few people permitted to address D'Alesio by his first name.

"With all the excitement about the Colorado bombing, and given the play it's gotten in the presidential campaign, I figured I'd take a look at the analysis coming out of the Bureau about the incident," Baines said.

"I thought the FBI said that there wasn't much doubt about who was behind it," responded D'Alesio.

"You're right, that's what the report said. But imagine my surprise when I found out the Bureau never sent a man out there to investigate. Their conclusions are based solely on the press accounts."

"Are you sure? That makes absolutely no sense, Baines."

"Yes, sir. Here's the report of the agent assigned to the case." Baines handed D'Alesio a thin sheaf of papers. "It refers to the Denver newspaper's account of what happened, plus the call into the paper of responsibility by a DOE member. But you'll see, that's it. No firsthand investigating."

"That's quite unusual. Maybe the agent thought it was an open-and-shut case, and there was no need to visit the site."

"Could have been, Rick, but that would have violated all forms of protocol. And what surprised me even more is that no satellite photos were referenced."

"Did we have any 'birds' over the area at the time of the bombing?"

"I checked, and we did have one over the mountain states at the time. Strange thing, though—it was turned off during the hour of the bombing, so we've got no pictures."

"Now that's very strange. Though the birds sometimes go dark for routine maintenance, don't they?"

"Yes, they do, but usually another bird does back-up duty for the period when the satellite goes dark for maintenance. In this case, nothing."

"Did you call the NSA?"

"I did, but you know they never return my calls."

"Yes, Baines, they feel like they're a kingdom unto

their own. But I wouldn't be too concerned about all this. Probably some foul-up in the satellite scheduling."

"But Rick, given the Bureau's conclusion that it was a 'slam-dunk' that DOE was behind the bombing, don't you think it should've soft-pedaled its conclusions somewhat, given that we've got virtually nothing to go on?"

"Hold on, Baines. I thought the bombing fit the M.O. of DOE all the way."

"That's what I thought too, until I figured out that the explosives used in the blast were more powerful than anything DOE has ever used. That's based on the extent of the blast and fire destruction at the ski lodge, using photos from Google Earth."

D'Alesio's demeanor quickly changed. "So what are you saying?"

"I'm not concluding anything, but this is very suspicious. I imagine the trail's gone cold now, so we'll never know if someone did the bombing and then pointed the finger at DOE."

D'Alesio got up to leave. "It's time for our meeting," he said. "And in the meantime, you keep your suspicions to yourself."

Baines was taken aback by D'Alesio's abruptness, as his boss usually encouraged him to follow all leads. He followed him to the NSC meeting, which D'Alesio was chairing. The President wasn't in attendance this time, though the Vice President was.

The meeting started with a brief discussion of the situation in Morocco. Morocco had long been a stable, if undemocratic, ally of the United States. But with warming temperatures in North Africa, Morocco's economy was under severe stress. Unemployment had risen to more than 25%, and with it Islamic fundamentalists were threatening the regime. Radical Islamic groups had gone underground in the 2020s but re-emerged as Morocco's economic woes got worse. Blaming the West—and by association, Morocco's rulers—for climate change, the Islamic groups were organizing large protests by shop owners and university students. D'Alesio worried that the pro-U.S. king might have to capitulate if the situation didn't improve soon.

D'Alesio next asked the Secretary of State about "the Canadian issue." The Canadian embassy and consulates had recently imposed a visa requirement for travel to Canada by Americans, creating an embarrassing flap for the administration. An increasing number of American visitors to Canada were not returning home, and the suspicion was that the displaced, farmers and others figured that Canada was a safe haven from the tumult of global warming.

The Secretary of State reported that the Canadian ambassador had promised to lift the visa requirement through December as a favor to the President, but there were no promises after then. D'Alesio frowned, but said that would have to do.

The discussion then turned to the forest fires out west. Each fire season had become worse than the preceding one. Over the years, fires had blackened up to one-third of the forests in some Western states. Fires covering more than 500,000 acres were not uncommon. As with many other natural disasters, global warming had contributed to the problem. The temperature rise of two degrees had caused

Dana M. Stein

early snow melt in the mountains, leading to an earlier start to the fire season. The higher temperatures had also reduced humidity levels and dried out forest brush, both of which made the fires larger and harder to control.

This time there was concern that the fire season seemed to have no end. Usually, by the end of October, all fires were under control and diminishing in size. But this time, new fires had erupted in California, Nevada, and Wyoming. The fire that was getting the most media play was the 300,000 acre blaze in Yellowstone National Park that was out of control. The Vice President asked D'Alesio if there were any remaining fire crews that could be deployed to Yellowstone, and D'Alesio said all units were stretched thin. D'Alesio worried that with fire crews having worked around the clock for months, there was risk of an accident and loss of life. The Vice President reminded D'Alesio that a fire in one of the nation's most popular parks wasn't good for the President, prompting Baines to wonder if there was *any* issue that didn't have a political dimension.

One of the NSC members asked about the status of the gas-engine legislation on Capitol Hill. D'Alesio replied that though the Senate Environment and Public Works Committee had approved it, the bill was facing the threat of a filibuster in the Senate. The Vice President commented that a filibuster wouldn't be so bad, but that even if the bill passed, he'd be surprised if the President signed it. At that point, he turned to Baines and said, "Unless, Mr. Baines, you have anything contrary to say on the issue." Startled, Baines felt the eyes of everyone in the room turn to him. Baines just shook his head and was glad to have the meeting end soon after.

Chapter 19

It was during the DOE leadership meeting in Albuquerque that the rally in Washington had been planned. Typical of DOE's method of operating, it was organized furtively. Word quickly got out to DOE's community and campus chapters without the major media outlets finding out. Once DOE announced the rally on October 19, six days before the event, other environmental groups were encouraged to join in. DOE said that it wanted the rally to be the largest environmental gathering in Washington's history.

October 25th was a bright, crisp Saturday. The hot spell that had characterized much of the early autumn was now over, and most of the area's trees still had remnants of traditional fall foliage. Hundreds of buses poured into Washington, and by 9 a.m. the first rally goers had started to crowd onto the Mall.

Just as he did every day, Baines checked in on his

father that morning. At first he was worried when he couldn't find his father at his tent, but his tent-mate said that his father was busy helping the rally organizers set up. Baines was relieved when he finally found his father near the Lincoln Memorial, lugging electronic equipment that was being set up on the steps of the Memorial.

His father was tired and covered with sweat. "Dad, you should take it easy. There are plenty of young folks around here who can do the heavy lifting."

"Don't worry. I'm so excited about this rally, I feel like I'm forty years younger. Besides, shouldn't you be worried about being seen with these folks? I'm sure the park police are watching."

Baines frowned. "I doubt I'm the only government official who's interested in seeing what's going to happen today. You have your meds with you?" Baines referred to the nitroglycerine that his dad carried around, in case of cardiac emergency. His father had had two minor heart attacks over the past five years.

"Yup, I never leave home without 'em," he said, tapping his shirt pocket. "Just let me be, go check in with your bosses at the White House, and then come back to hear what the people have to say."

"If that's what you recommend, Dad, I'll be sure to do it." They hugged and went their separate ways.

By 1 p.m., the crowd on the Mall was overflowing. As park police helicopters hovered overhead, the crowd developed an almost festive air. Rally participants had brought colorful streamers and signs that identified the groups they were associated with—DOE, the Sierra Club, the Nature Preservation Society, the Chesapeake Bay Defender Coalition, and others. They crowded around the reflecting pool in front of the Lincoln Memorial and spilled over into adjacent parts of the Mall.

A little after 1 p.m., several men and women came to the dais. A bearded man with a slight build walked to the podium and began to speak.

"Good afternoon, fellow citizens of the earth. My name is Andy Rowan, and I am chairman of the group known as the Defenders of Earth." The crowd's members, many of whom had been talking with friends or family, grew quiet.

"Along with other leaders of Defenders of Earth, I am here at great risk to my personal safety. We do not know if, at the end of this rally, we will be arrested and taken into custody by federal marshals.

"But we are here because our planet is in a state of emergency. We have no time to waste. After decades of insufficient action by our leaders, we stand united in our demand for dramatic measures that will stem the tide of global warming and save our cities and coastlines from being inundated.

"Your presence here today is proof that the people understand that the time for half-measures that tinker with our carbon footprint is over. Yet our leaders do not fully understand this, despite working in a city whose summers are hotter, whose river has risen, and whose cherry blossoms bloom a month earlier than they used to.

"So, on behalf of all citizens of our planet, and the generations who will come after us, we demand major action. And we do so while renouncing the use of any means that involve violence in any way." The crowd, which had applauded Rowan's remarks several times, got very quiet.

"The Defenders of Earth announce this end to violence because we have concluded that peaceful means are the only way to advance our cause and to protect the earth. We also do this because the tragic bombing in Colorado, for which we are not—I repeat, are not—culpable, shows that our opponents will use reprehensible tactics to try to undercut our cause.

"No more will the Defenders of Earth operate in the shadows. Through this rally, we announce our desire to join forces with the other excellent organizations represented on this podium, and to try to save the earth in its time of peril."

The crowd cheered lustily. Rowan was then joined at the podium by several other environmental leaders, who joined hands and jointly announced the creation of a national Green Party, to be chaired by the head of the Sierra Club. The rally ended with the leaders exhorting the crowd to head to the Senate, which was debating the gas-engine legislation, and demand passage of the bill.

Baines, who was standing next to a tree not too far from the podium, found himself in the midst of a tide of rally goers who were headed to the Capitol. After being swept along for a couple of hundred feet, he finally was able to break free. All throughout the speech, Baines had been conveying his impressions of the rally to D'Alesio with the latest in telecommunications technology. He had whispered his comments to an ear piece, which translated his words into text that appeared on D'Alesio's hand-held device.

With the rally over, he called in to D'Alesio with his

final report. Rowan's speech had been short but powerful, Baines said, and his renunciation of violence meant
that DOE could no longer be used as a bogeyman. As to
whether the new Green Party would be a political threat,
he was skeptical. D'Alesio thanked him and told him to
come to the office when he could. As Baines hung up with
D'Alesio, he grimaced as he saw several plainclothes policemen arrest Rowan and take him to a waiting police car.

Dana M. Stein

Chapter 20

Not knowing what his destination would be, Harper headed west in Nebraska on Route 2. When he approached the outskirts of Lincoln, he stopped at the first Walmart he saw. He was hungry and since he had left Waubonsie in a hurry, he needed to pick up a few odds and ends.

After he had a grilled cheese sandwich at the store's lunch counter, he took a look around at the mammoth store. The store sold almost every conceivable product that anyone would ever need to buy. After he'd filled up his pickup with biodiesel—most of Walmart's stores in the Midwest had biodiesel filling stations—he started wandering around. Walmart had recently started to sell cars at some of its stores, including the one at Lincoln, so Harper took a look at the latest models. Several auto companies sold sleek new pickups and compact cars. GM's new hybrid pickup had solar panels embedded in the truck's flatbed, and Ford's new cars used the latest in lightweight plastic and metal composites. Toyota sold a popular battery-powered, "plug-in" car that could be recharged at electrical filling stations and got an average of 300 miles per charge.

Harper thought he'd love to get the Toyota plug-in model. He smiled as he imagined the story he'd tell the sales agent about his sources of income. "Well, you know, sir, I used to have a thriving farm until temperatures got out of hand. And then I had good prospects for growing corn out of a state park in Iowa until my land got torn up. And my son makes a decent living, but unfortunately, I don't know quite where he is. Aside from the fact that I have no tillable land and no home at present, I'm an excellent credit risk."

Harper went into the camping section of the store and looked for a pup tent. He figured that the next park he pulled into wouldn't have the same free cabins he'd had in Waubonsie, so he should prepare to rough it. He bought a small portable stove, some cooking utensils and a couple of flashlights. In his rush to leave Waubonsie, he'd had to leave his sleeping bag behind, so Harper bought one with fleece that he thought would keep him warm in the mountains. He also bought a dozen more rounds of ammunition for his .38, just in case he encountered anyone else who had Beasley's poor sense.

He loaded his cart with other odds and ends—some blankets, wool socks, toothpaste, a razor and twine. As he waited in the checkout line, out of curiosity, he checked the country of origin of all the things he had. Not one had been made in the U.S., and he figured that was the case

Dana M. Stein

with about 95% of the items in the store. Harper thought that just as imports had eliminated most of U.S. manufacturing, the warming was starting to wipe out the one thing the country had done well for hundreds of years—growing crops, and lots of them.

He loaded his items into his truck, and sat in the front seat. *What to do, now?* He could head west, toward where his son was waging war on fire. But what would he say to his son, if Harper found him. Son, I'm at the end of my rope and have nowhere to go. All I've got left is you and what I stowed in this pickup. Harper couldn't imagine saying those things to Brian, let alone what Brian's reaction would be.

So he started his pickup and pulled out of the parking lot. Within minutes he had gotten onto the interstate just west of Lincoln. Somehow, seeing the other cars on the road was mildly reassuring. He could pretend that with all of those drivers headed somewhere with purpose, that he had somewhere to go as well.

He knew he had to call Brian, but he couldn't bring himself to do it. So he promised himself that he'd call after he reached the exit for Grand Island. Then it was the exit for Kearney, then North Platte, then Ogallala. The only good thing about his inner debate, he thought, was that it made the miles pass quickly.

After Ogallala, Harper left the interstate and headed northwest into the Nebraska panhandle along Route 26. As he got close to Scottsbluff, he did a quick detour to visit the Scotts Bluff National Monument, which he'd wanted to see since he was a kid. The two bluffs, Scotts Bluff and South Bluff, seemed to lord over the North Platte River and everything around it. A path marker for several trails, including the Oregon and Pony Express trails, the bluffs had witnessed many waves of western-bound travelers. If the bluffs could talk, he wondered, would they think that the warming was a bigger change than anything they'd seen over the centuries? A hundred years from now, Harper thought, the bluffs and the prairie in the monument area probably won't look very different. Parts of Iowa, though, will likely be much different—will they look like the grass-covered prairie, or will they be dry like the badlands that lay in between Scotts Bluff and the river? Harper felt fortunate that he wouldn't be around to find out.

After all the commotion and traveling of the day, Harper was tired. The sun was almost setting as he saw the signs for a campground and pulled into the Lake Minatare State Recreation Area. He was so weary that after he set up his tent and rolled out his sleeping bag, he fell asleep on top of the bag with his clothes and shoes on. But the Nebraska panhandle's elevation was much greater than Iowa's, so the chilly evening air woke him up in the middle of the night. He pulled out his blankets and tried to fall back asleep, but he was wide awake. Finally, Harper turned on his cell phone and switched it to a twenty-four hour news station. What he saw was upsetting.

There were new wildfires in Southern California. The National Guard had been called up to help fight the fires and provide relief to the beleaguered firefighters. The day before, a helicopter had crashed as it delivered firefighters to a blaze that was threatening an upscale development on a ridge. Whether it was strong winds or pilot

Dana M. Stein

fatigue that had caused the crash, no one knew, but at least two men had died. The flames were so fast-moving that several residents had to hide overnight in a riverbed that had dried up years ago. Harper thought that for those poor residents, who had been rescued at the last minute, Dante's inferno had come to life.

The only silver lining to all this news was that there was nothing about the Yellowstone fire. That wasn't much comfort to Harper, however, and he tossed and turned the rest of the night.

At daybreak, Harper realized he had to call his son. He couldn't put it off anymore. He had to call Brian to let him know he was coming to Yellowstone—for how long or to do what, he didn't know, just that he was coming.

So he pulled out his cell phone, and dialed Brian. No answer, just automatic rollover into his voice mail. He left a message saying that he would show up in Yellowstone by that afternoon.

By the time he passed Casper, Wyoming, Harper had stopped looking at the scenery. He just wanted to get to Yellowstone. Normally, he would have stopped to admire Wyoming's natural beauty, especially as he crossed the Shoshrong National Forest in the final approach to Yellowstone. But it was of no interest to Harper at this point.

As he entered Yellowstone, he could see where the fire was raging. He got to where the firefighters had set up camp and parked his truck. Most everyone had the same worried expression that the farmers in Bloomfield, Iowa, seemed to have the day that Harper left his farm, except this time two groups were rushing about. When he found out why, he almost fell down.

The hotshot unit that Brian was in had been overrun. The winds in Yellowstone had been whipping the fire back and forth, and while the unit had built what they thought was a strong firewall, the fire had leapt across treetops and swept across the ridge they were on. Radio contact had been lost for an hour, until the call came in that they all had survived, though two were badly burned. They had all sought refuge under their protective aluminum shrouds, designed as a last-resort protection against approaching fire. Two rescue crews were now scrambling to get their gear together and head out in jeeps.

Harper asked if he could join the others in their wait for the crews to return. He sat on an overturned bucket, watching the electronic map that showed the progress of the rescuers. What was a half-hour wait seemed endless. Finally, the jeeps returned with the members of the battered unit.

Two were on stretchers and so heavily bandaged as to be unrecognizable. As soon as the jeeps stopped, the stretchers were quickly carried to a waiting helicopter, which took off in an instant. The other eighteen men and women—blackened from head to toe with soot and sweat—slowly stepped out of the jeeps.

Harper anxiously scanned their faces. He didn't see Brian among them. But as they headed toward the medics' tents, one man broke away and came toward Harper.

"Hi, Dad." Brian came up to Harper and hugged him. Harper wouldn't let him go.

"Oh sweet Jesus, Brian, you're okay!"

"A few minor burns, but other than that I'm alright."

"I can't even recognize you!"

"Having a close encounter with a wildfire does tend to change your appearance."

"What about the two they took away? Were you friends with them?"

"Everyone in our unit is tight with everyone. They've got a fifty/fifty chance of making it."

"I'm so, so sorry. But you're my son, and just thank God you came out of this." Harper's eyes welled up with tears.

"Dad, you always did embarrass me. Listen, I've got to be checked out by a medic. Stick around for an hour or so, and I'll come find you."

"I'll be here. I'm not going anywhere."

As his son walked away, a feeling of intense weariness came over Harper. At first he thought about getting his sleeping bag out, but instead he walked to the nearest field and just lay down in the grass. He looked up at the blue sky above, obscured to the north by billowing clouds of smoke. His head was spinning from relief at seeing his son alive.

The next thing he knew, Brian was standing over him.

"Dad, you have a nice nap? No one knew where you'd gone."

"Oh, sorry. The medics check you out?"

"Sure did. Said that there's nothing that a few days off won't cure. You want to go to the mess hall with me? The boss said that if you drove all the way up here to see the fire, you're welcome to share a few meals."

"Would love to."

After a huge meal, family-style—Harper wondered

where the firefighters could put all that they ate—Harper and Brian took a long walk. They found the listening spot for Yellowstone's wolves, and after an hour of waiting, they heard the wolves make their plaintive cries.

They continued their walk the next morning. They ambled alongside the bison, who seemed oblivious to their presence and the commotion that the fires were causing. After a while, they started talking about the future. Harper told his son how he'd left the farm behind and about the debacle at Waubonsie. Harper said he had no clue as to where he'd go or what he'd do, but he was open to suggestions.

Brian shared that the near-death experience he'd had on the ridge had shaken him. He had thought he'd make a career out of the fire service, but after having seen his two friends nearly die, he wasn't so sure. One thing he was sure about, however, was that he didn't want him and his dad to be apart anymore. They were the only family they had, and after nearly dying under an aluminum shroud, he felt they should be together.

Harper was so overcome that he didn't know what to say. He loved his son very much, but Harper was embarrassed by the situation he was in. He had always been the head of the family, but now he had virtually nothing.

When he expressed his self-doubt to Brian, Brian told him that he had a job for him. It might not earn any money, but it would be helping a lot of people. Brian's base camp was in the middle of California, where wildfires had displaced several hundred people during the summer. Right now, the displaced were living out of trailers until they were permanently relocated. They were trying to grow vegetables to supplement the poor food rations they were getting from FEMA, but no one in the group had a green thumb.

"Ah, so you want me to be a consultant on growing victory gardens," Harper asked, referring to the backyard gardens that people grew during World War II.

"Sure, Dad. You always did grow the best squash and cucumbers in our backyard. Probably no one knows how to put together a raised garden bed like you do."

"And where will I stay?"

"You stay with me. I'm gone about half the time, on jaunts to fight fires hither and yon, but the rest of the time, if you don't butt heads with me too much, you can sleep on the cot in the spare room."

Harper thought for a moment. All his life, he'd wanted to do something to make a difference. His farm co-op board had been a waste of time, and the 4-H club he'd worked with had disbanded as school kids realized there wasn't much future in farming. And in recent years, he'd just been focused on surviving. With what Brian was proposing, he might be able to help people who, like him, had had their world turn upside down.

"Well, I always wanted to see California."

"That sounds good. Now if you don't mind, can we head over to the woods across the field? I think I just saw a few moose cubs with their mama taking a drink in the creek."

Chapter 21

November first will be a historic day, Baines thought as he got dressed early that morning. The Senate, influenced by the crush of visitors it got after the environmental rally, had beaten back the threat of a filibuster and passed the gas engine bill on October thirtieth. Much to everyone's surprise, the President had announced the next day that he would sign the legislation. Baines was thrilled, though most of his fellow NSC members were most displeased. There was much speculation as to why the President was going to sign the legislation—some thought it was because by now he was consistently, if narrowly, ahead in the polls; others thought that he wanted to throttle the formation of the new Green Party. Whatever the reason, Baines was happy that the President seemed to show some backbone in the face of opposition from the auto industry and the Defense

Dana M. Stein

Department. The bill signing was scheduled for 10 a.m. that morning in the Rose Garden of the White House.

Baines hadn't had the chance to visit his father since the rally, so he made sure he had the time to visit that morning. When he initially couldn't find his father, he wasn't overly concerned, as he had had to chase him down the morning of the rally. But when he saw his father's tent-mate with a look of concern, he grew apprehensive.

"Jimmy, where's my dad?" Baines asked.

"He didn't call you?"

"No."

"The day after the rally, he woke up with chest pains and was rushed to the hospital."

"Which one?"

"George Washington, I think."

"Is he all right?"

"Turns out he suffered a heart attack, but he's stable, at least as of yesterday."

"A heart attack?" Baines was incredulous. "Omigod, I didn't know. Thanks very much, Jimmy."

Baines took off across the Mall in a dead run. He was quite a sight, sprinting with his jacket on and tie flying. He made it to George Washington University Hospital in about ten minutes, wheezing. His father was still in the intensive care unit and visiting hours hadn't started, but with his White House badge, he prevailed upon the nurse at the desk to let him see his father.

His father was awake and seemed a little embarrassed. "Son, I'm sorry I didn't call you."

"Sorry? Dad, I had to find out from Jimmy. I almost had an aneurysm when I heard."

"I said I was sorry."

"It's okay. How are you feeling?"

"The doctor said I had a heart attack. Must have been due to the stress and excitement of the previous day. That was some rally, wasn't it!"

"It sure was. Dad, I told you not to overdo it."

"I didn't think I had, but after traipsing around Capitol Hill with everyone else that day, I came back to the Mall feeling pretty tired. And then the next morning, I woke up feeling like a Mack truck was sitting on my chest. The ambulance came pretty fast, and here I am."

"How serious was the heart attack?"

"Not too bad, they say. I suffered some damage to the heart muscle, but they said I'll be okay."

"How long before you're discharged?"

"I dunno, maybe a day or two. Maybe with your clout, you can get me out of here pretty soon."

"Dad, even though winters in D.C. aren't so bad anymore, you know that a cardiac patient shouldn't spend winter camped out on the National Mall."

"Yeah, you and the doctor must be colluding."

"Colluding?" Baines was a little angry. "Among the three of us, he and I are the only ones with any common sense!"

"Calm down, son. I was just kidding."

"I hope so. You know that you've got to leave the Mall. My invitation's still open."

"As much as I hate to say it, I guess…"

"You guess I'm right?"

Dana M. Stein

"Don't make me say it, but well, okay, yes."

"So you'll move in with me?"

"I suppose. I was getting kind of tired of that tent, anyway. Jimmy's a pretty bad snorer, and I never could cook worth a damn."

Baines smiled with relief. "You mean with your fancy sun-powered microwave, you couldn't make gourmet meals?"

"At least I know I can cook better than you."

"Well, you're finally going to find out. I'll make arrangements to pick you up when you're discharged and move your belongings to my place."

"Okay, son. But understand it's nothing permanent. Just until I can find other quarters."

"You stay as long as you like, or until you drive me crazy."

"Deal."

Baines left the hospital feeling relieved. Although he was sorry that a heart attack had been the cause, he was happy that his father would be moving in. He could keep track of him, make sure he got the care he needed, and Baines's early morning jaunts to the Mall would be over.

He looked at his watch, and realized that he was in danger of missing the bill signing. So once again he started running, this time toward the White House. He realized he looked a little bedraggled as he approached the security desk at the White House, with his tie awry and face completely flushed from his two dashes that morning. He managed to get to the Rose Garden just in time.

D'Alesio was the first to see him. "What the hell happened to you this morning?"

"Long story. My dad's in the hospital, but he'll be okay."

"Sorry about your father. All the kinks were worked out with the signing statement for the bill?"

"Yes." Baines thought that if it was a choice between the condition of his father's health and that of the signing statement, D'Alesio surely would opt for the signing statement.

The Rose Garden was packed with reporters and environmental advocates. Rowan had been released from police custody without charges the day before, but he wasn't there, much to Baines's relief. The President looked as happy as he'd ever been. Baines thought that the decisiveness he'd shown with the bill had done him good.

The Vice President wasn't there, however. "Where's the Veep?" Baines asked of D'Alesio.

"Claims he's sick and couldn't make it."

"That's pretty odd, isn't it?" Baines replied. D'Alesio just shrugged.

Baines returned that afternoon to the hospital to check in on his father. His dad had watched the bill signing on television, and they chatted about it. For the first time Baines could remember, his father said good things about the President. He couldn't disagree with his father's assessment that the President's spine seemed to have stiffened. They talked more about his father moving in. For the first time in a long while, Baines felt that he and his father were connecting and supporting each other.

As Baines left the hospital late in the day, he realized he still had work to do. This time, however, he could return to the White House in a leisurely walk. When he checked in, most people had left, including D'Alesio. He turned on the television set in his office and watched the evening news and talk shows. Most of the prognosticators seemed to think that the President's action had sealed his re-election chances. Baines thought that was good; he'd have a job for another four years. He also was hopeful that, with the President's newfound decisiveness, they could turn a corner on climate change.

He cleaned up some files on his desk. He found Margolis's phone number among his papers, and thought about calling her to set up that post-election get-together. Was this going to be a date, or just a friendly chat? It was nice to have the luxury of thinking about these things, he thought.

Just as he picked up the phone, he heard some rumbling outside. Something very heavy was moving down the street, heavy enough to cause the hallway chandeliers to shake. He and the few others in the building ran to the entranceway, and couldn't believe what they saw. An M-2 tank had moved down Pennsylvania Avenue, stopped in front of the Old Executive Office Building and pointed its gun turret at the building. Baines was stunned. He quickly called D'Alesio on his cell phone, but he didn't answer.

A few minutes later, a squad of soldiers took up position outside the entrance to the building. A limousine appeared, and out hopped D'Alesio. He joined one of the soldiers, and the two of them came to the entrance. D'Alesio pointed to Baines, but refused to make eye contact with him.

The soldier, dressed in a crisp green uniform and with a handgun at his side, spoke in clipped tones to Baines. "Mr. Michael Baines. On orders of the Vice President, now acting President, I am placing you under arrest. Please follow me." Baines's head was spinning, but he managed to ask why he was being arrested. The soldier told him he'd find out very shortly. Baines looked at D'Alesio, who still wouldn't look at him, and without any further protest, he followed them out into the November night.

Dana M. Stein

CPSIA information can be obtained at www.ICGtesting.com
Printed in the USA
LVOW06s0235160115

423073LV00001B/117/P